D1210205

LICHEE TREE

LICHEE TREE

by Ching Yeung Russell

decorations by Christopher Zhong-Yuan Zhang

BOYDS MILLS PRESS

Special thanks to my husband, Phillip Russell,
and my editor, Karen Klockner,
with whose help this book is made possible.

Text copyright © 1997 by Christina Ching Yeung Russell
Illustrations copyright © 1997 by Boyds Mills Press

Published by Caroline House
Boyds Mills Press, Inc.
A Highlights Company
815 Church Street
Honesdale, Pennsylvania 18431
Printed in the United States of America

Publisher Cataloging-in-Publication Data
Russell, Ching Yeung.
Lichee tree / by Ching Yeung Russell ; illustrated by Christopher Zhong-Yuan
Zhang.—1st ed.
[156]p. : ill. ; cm.
Summary : Ten-year-old Ying can't wait for her lichee tree to bloom so she can sell the
fruit for money to help her family.
ISBN 1-56397-629-3
1. Fruit trees—Fiction—Juvenile literature. 2. Family life—China—Fiction—Juvenile
literature. [1. Fruit trees—Fiction. 2. Family life—China—Fiction.] I. Zhang,
Christopher Zhong-Yuan, ill. II. Title.
853.54 [F]—dc20   1997   AC   CIP
Library of Congress Catalog Card Number 96-84678

First edition, 1997
Book designed by Jean Krulis
The text of this book is set in 12.5 Berkeley Book

1 3 5 7 9 10 8 6 4 2

To my loving sons,
Jeremy and Jonathan,
and to Joanna Lee,
for her help and friendship.

LICHEE TREE

1

Below us, acre after acre of tender, green rice plants stretched as far as I could see. The branch of the Pearl River that flowed by our town like a skinny snake sparkled in the April afternoon sun, dazzling my eyes like thousands of diamonds disappearing at the horizon.

We were sitting on a huge, granite boulder on top of Buddhist Hill, taking a break after raking dried weeds for cooking fuel.

I shaded my eyes with my hand and searched the far reaches of the bowl-shaped sky. Even though I felt the city of Canton was way beyond the sky—a place that no one I knew could ever see or reach—I asked my twelve-year old cousin Kee, "Do you know where Canton is?"

"Canton?" Kee scratched his head and thought for a few seconds, then pointed to his left. "I think that way."

"No, it's that way," said Ah Man, pointing the opposite way. Kee's good friend was also in the sixth grade.

"I don't think so. Canton is supposed to be located northwest of Tai Kong. It should be that way."

Ah Man shrugged his shoulders and mumbled, "I'm not sure. But what does it matter? We'll never get there, anyway."

"It would be nice to live there," Kee said, dreaming.

"It has everything," Ah Man declared.

"Everything? How about beads?" I asked.

I was crazy about colorful, sparkling beads and longed for some to make a ring or a necklace, but no one sold beads in our small town.

"I guess," Kee replied.

"What do you mean, 'I guess'?" Ah Man said. "Of course they do! They even have *kwailos*!"

"*Kwailos*?" I turned to Ah Man. I had learned from schoolbooks that big cities had hospitals, buses, trains, and factories, but I never thought they might have *kwailos*. *Kwailos* lived far away, on the other side of the world.

"Mr. Hon said there are," Ah Man and Kee both replied.

"How does Mr. Hon know?" I paid close attention.

Kee said, "Mr. Hon is *from* Canton, remember?"

Mr. Hon was their literature teacher, but he was substituting for Mrs. Yu, our fourth-grade teacher, while she was absent.

2

"Did Mr. Hon hear them speak? Do they really talk like *gee-gee, goo-goo*?"

"I guess so. That's what everyone says."

"How about their writing? Does it really look like chicken intestines, long and curved so you can't tell the head from the tail?"

Ah Man gave me a disgusted look and said, "Of course, dummy! Everyone knows that!"

I ignored him and kept questioning Kee, because I had heard so many funny things about *kwailos*: they talked funny, they wrote funny, they dressed funny. They even grew long hair on their pink bodies, like monkeys!

"Did Mr. Hon say why *kwailos* love to bundle themselves up even in the summer? Are they afraid of getting sunburned, or are they trying to cover up their hairy bodies?"

"No. It is some kind of uniform, some kind of religion. What is it called?" Kee turned to Ah Man.

Ah Man rolled his eyes, "Who cares about the *kwailos*? Why don't you ask Mr. Hon yourself!" He picked up a small rock and threw it as far as he could, because he didn't know the answer.

I didn't want them to know my secret, but I didn't like Ah Man's attitude. So I boasted, "I don't need to ask Mr. Hon! I will go there to see them with my own eyes someday!"

"Hey, wake up, wake up!" Kee said. "You are dreaming again."

"No, I'm not. How many times have you said I was dreaming? When I grow up and get rich, I will go!"

"Get rich!" Ah Man rolled his eyes again. He had never liked me. I had come to live with Kee and his family at Chan Village when I was five. Kee's grandma, my Ah Pau, often told Kee to play with me so I wouldn't miss my own parents who lived in Hong Kong.

I fought back. "You never know! Maybe tomorrow a piece of gold will just drop right in front of me from the sky!"

They laughed, but I didn't. "You never can tell," I said.

"Time to go back to work," Kee reminded us.

I was the last one to get to my feet. I was still searching with my eyes for where Canton was supposed to be.

After we raked for a while, the boys' baskets were full and they decided to quit. Mine was still only half full. I didn't insist on staying longer to rake more dried weeds. Ah Pau had never complained that I didn't bring enough home. We each carried our own basket. We used the ends of our rakes as walking sticks, carefully climbing down the hill, with the baskets on our backs.

The sun was gradually heading toward the West. Ah Man suggested, "Let's take the shortcut. I'm tired and hungry."

"Are you kidding?" answered Kee. "I don't want to go by Ghost Walk's sugarcane field!"

I was glad Kee disagreed. I feared even mentioning Ghost Walk's name. He was the town bully. No one

4

could stop him from doing bad things to other people. So we went home by the regular route. As we neared home, I didn't see Ah Pau, who usually sat on the stone bench at the intersection outside of Chan Village waiting for us at the end of the day. She was always anxious to see us come home in one piece.

"Ah Pau is not there!" I said, feeling a little uneasy. Not waiting for Kee to answer, I picked up my pace.

"Ah Pau!"

2

When I got to our front courtyard, I stopped short. We had a visitor.

A fat lady who was dressed very nicely was at our house. I was relieved to see Ah Pau. Auntie was there, too. Almost immediately I noticed a box of cookies on the table. The cookies were a gift from the lady. This meant we would have cookies to eat after she left!

The lady was sipping her tea and talking about something enthusiastically: ". . . she can be happy and wealthy all her life." I didn't know what she was talking about, and I didn't care. I was only interested in the cookies—I was always hungry.

I looked at Ah Pau and Auntie. To my surprise, they seemed very worried. Auntie kept smoking her water pipe nervously. Ah Pau acted as if her mind was a thousand miles away. She didn't even know that I was there. Seeing that, I did not greet them as I usually did. I walked straight to the backyard.

As I passed by my room, I heard someone's muffled crying. I stuck my head in to see who it was. Ah So, Kee's seventeen-year-old sister, was hiding behind the door crying.

I went inside and whispered, "What's wrong? Who's that lady?"

She motioned me to go, but I didn't. Instead, I stayed there for a while, still wondering what was going on. I saw Kee go into the backyard. I left Ah So to follow him and asked, "Hey, who's that lady?"

"How do *I* know?" He dumped his dried weeds at one corner of the backyard, and I did the same.

"How come Ah So is crying?"

"You think I will believe you again? Not long ago you told me she was holding a needle in the air and just smiling, not doing any embroidery. Now you tell me she's crying. Do you think I'm a three-year-old who will believe whatever you say?"

"Go and see for yourself! She is hiding in my room!"

"I don't stoop so low as to spy on everybody, like you do!"

I stamped away.

The fat lady was standing up, ready to leave. At one end of the daybed, Auntie was still smoking her silver water pipe. She seemed not to notice that the guest was going to leave. Ah Pau glanced at the cookies on the table, picked up the box, and gave it to the guest, saying, "Please take it back. We appreciate the thought."

"No, no, no. This is just a little something." She stuck it back in Ah Pau's hand, but Ah Pau still tried to insist that she take it.

I wished Ah Pau wouldn't do that. She and the fat lady pushed the box back and forth, like they were playing a game of tug of war. Finally, the lady saw me. She lost her patience, grabbed the box, and slammed it on the table, declaring, "I don't have time to play games with you. Just take it for the children!" As she was crossing the threshold with her short legs, she turned and lowered her voice, saying to Auntie, "It's a good chance. Think about it. You don't seem to realize how powerful he is." Without waiting for Auntie to say anything in response, she left.

I ran to the backyard and reported to Kee, "The fat lady left cookies for us!"

Kee didn't accuse me of making it up this time. He said, "Great! I'm hungry!"

"Me, too!"

We ran back to the living room. Auntie, who seemed even more worried now that the fat lady had left, saw that Kee was moving toward the box, ready to open it. She shouted in a voice I had never heard before, "Why are you so immature? Big trouble is coming. We don't know if we will live or die, but all you want to do is eat, eat, eat and play, play, play!" She started coughing.

Neither Kee nor I knew what kind of big trouble was coming, but I knew it must be serious. That evening Ah So didn't come down to cook supper as she usually did. Auntie had to cook, but she made only two dishes. There were some dried fish and some vegetables. Ah So didn't come down to offer incense to the kitchen god, earth god, and heaven god before we ate. I had to take her place. She didn't even come down to eat. During the meal, which was way past our regular suppertime, Auntie and Ah Pau ate very little and hardly spoke. When Kee put down his chopsticks, Auntie told him to go and tell Uncle to come home as soon as possible.

When Uncle came home, all three adults went upstairs for a "grown-up's business talk" that neither Kee nor I could join.

3

Auntie was wrong. We didn't have any big trouble as she said we would. Ah So seemed even happier than before, often humming Cantonese opera when she was doing her embroidery or cooking. She had been going out in the evening lately.

Everything seemed normal.

The following Sunday morning, Ah Mei, Ah Won, and I were on our way home. We had been looking for beads at the theater, where a Cantonese opera troupe had been performing the night before. We always went to search the stage after the opera left. We never had much luck, though, because all the other girls in town also went there to search. I had found only two sequins, one bugle bead, and five seed beads since I started collecting a whole year ago.

Kee had heard me complaining that my collection was not even enough for a ring for my little finger. "Stupid!"

he said. "Why don't you look *under* the stage!"

I thought he was just teasing me at first. Then I asked him why there would be beads there.

"First," he said, "when the janitor sweeps the stage, he may sweep beads down through the cracks, and they will fall on the ground. Second, nobody else is as smart as me, so they won't think about the possibility of beads being down there. The beads that fall will stay under there year after year, since no one will pick them up! Why don't you use your knucklehead and think?"

Maybe he was right, I thought. So I begged Ah Mei and Ah Won to go with me. Neither of them was as crazy about beads as I was.

But Kee didn't tell me that it was pitch-dark under the stage and smelled musty like a damp graveyard. Ah Mei sprained her ankle when she stepped on the moss growing on some broken bricks, and Ah Won almost wet her pants. She thought she heard noises coming from above, because the lady's restroom at the back of the theater was located where a funeral home used to be. We didn't find any beads.

"I swear I'll *never* go to that rotten place again," Ah Mei said, shuffling next to me. She was eleven, one year older than me but in the same class. Her usually neat, shiny pigtails were a mess.

"Me, either," declared Ah Won, whose hair looked like half a black coconut shell. Her name was originally Ah Pui. But her grandfather had discovered that her name sounded like the name of her great aunt who had passed away long ago. It was unlucky if your name, even the pronunciation, was the same as someone else in your family. So her grandfather had changed her name to Ah Won.

I felt bad about Ah Mei spraining her ankle and Ah Won almost wetting her pants. But I didn't say anything. I just pictured myself wearing a red satin dress with my shiny bead necklace. Then I said, "You may change your mind when you are actually wearing some shiny beads of your own."

"No way!" they said.

My spirits were sagging because I knew my friends wouldn't go under the stage with me anymore. I had to admit that it was spooky there, and there was no way I would go there all by myself. Still, it seemed like the only way I could get enough beads for a ring or a necklace. While I was thinking desperately, Ah Won suddenly distracted me. "Hey, look!" she said.

We had just turned down the street leading toward Chan Village. There were several children gathered in front of Lee Yee's house. At once, Ah Won and I picked up our pace. We heard noises and saw a couple of pedestrians who were just passing by, shaking their heads.

"I wonder what is happening at Yee's house," Ah Won said. Lee Yee was her classmate.

"What's happening?" I asked one of the boys. Now we heard screaming and crying inside.

With fear in his face, he whispered, "Ghost Walk."

"Ghost Walk?"

"Yes, with two other men."

"What are they doing?" Ah Won heard us, and she looked worried.

"I don't know," the boy replied, trying to peer inside from the door frame. Then he turned around abruptly, warning, "They are coming!"

Just at that moment, two men tried to drag out Ah Yee's father, who held onto the door frame tightly, refusing to let them drag him away. Ghost Walk came out. He was a very tall, thin man with unnaturally wide jaws that made him look cruel and mean. He wore a handsome dark blue satin *tong cheong sam* and a nice pair of *tong cheong hai*. A gold watch chain dangled from his upper pocket. He looked rich, but his sharp outfit didn't conceal his stooped shoulders or the menacing look of his pale face. He took the cigarette that was hanging from his mouth and ground the glowing tip into Yee's father's hand. Yee's father let out a cry and lost his grip on the door frame. We all backed away in horror. Yee's mother cried and begged them not to take her husband away.

"Come," someone ordered, grabbing my hand. It was Ah Pau. She lowered her voice and said, "You don't watch someone's misfortune for fun!" When she saw Ah Won and Ah Mei, she said, "You come, too."

We followed Ah Pau home. "I wasn't watching for fun," I said. "I just wanted to know what was happening."

"You are not afraid of getting into trouble, but I am," Ah Pau said. She walked away hastily as if she would really get into trouble if she didn't leave.

No one liked Ghost Walk, but I didn't know how I could get into trouble by just watching. I kept turning my head to look. Ghost Walk's people were dragging Yee's father down the street now. Ghost Walk was beside them. He walked like a ghost—he shuffled along on the front of his feet, with his heels not touching the ground. Ghost Walk—that's what townspeople called him behind his back. His real name was Go See Wong.

"What did Yee's father do? Did he do something wrong?" I asked Ah Pau. I didn't often play with Yee, but I hoped that they wouldn't hurt her father.

"Sometimes you don't need to do anything wrong. It depends on your luck," Ah Pau mumbled. Ah Won, Ah Mei, and I didn't understand what she meant.

4

We finished mid-term exams on Saturday. We felt free! It was unusually warm for the end of April. After supper and a bath, almost every schoolchild in Chan Village assembled at the intersection near the outside of the village. There was a dim electric light hanging way up on a pole.

Some children squatted down next to the light pole to play Chinese chess. Some took off their clogs to play hopscotch. Some of the older kids like Kee, Ah Tyim, Ah Man, Ah Mei, and me played "Soldiers Catch Thieves." There were not many pedestrians out since the stores closed before dark. We felt as if we had the whole town to ourselves.

A small wonton stand did business underneath the streetlight. The owner of the stand raised his voice in the quiet night once in a while calling, "Fresh shrimp wonton and noodles!" But his voice was often drowned out by our shouting, chasing, and running.

It was an exciting game. We had almost caught all the thieves and were about to win when Ah Man, the head of the thieves, denied being caught and quit. The game was called off. We sang, "Poor loser! Poor loser!" and watched Ah Man disappear in the dark. Still grumbling, we took a shortcut down a side street, and headed back to the intersection. It was darker than Tai Gai because the street was in a residential area.

"Hey, look!" Ah Tyim said. In the dark we could see a pair of lovers, one tall and the other about a foot shorter, walking hand in hand, about a hundred feet ahead of us. It was fun to watch the lovers, because we seldom saw couples holding hands in public.

Kee suddenly whispered, "Do you think I have the guts to run between them?"

"How?" Ah Tyim and I asked.

"I'll tell you all later. Want to bet?" he asked me.

"I don't believe you will do it," I said.

"If I do, you have to give me one cent. If I don't, then I'll give you one cent."

I thought for a second and agreed. So did Ah Tyim. Ah Won didn't bet—she didn't have any money. We all seemed to have forgotten about Ah Man, the poor loser.

Kee instructed me, "You pretend to chase me, but don't stop until I run between them."

"Me? What if they get mad at me?"

"They won't—they are dating. People who are dating

don't easily get angry in front of their girlfriends or boyfriends. Besides that, I'm the one running between them, not you."

I thought he made sense, so I agreed.

I waited for Kee to run about five yards and then I pretended to chase him. He ran like crazy—then he dashed between the couple. They were so preoccupied with each other that they didn't even know Kee was running behind them. When he hit them, they almost tripped. Kee didn't stop. He kept running until he was out of sight. I still pretended to chase him, but the couple went back together and seemed unconcerned about Kee's rudeness.

When I was almost to the end of the alley, Kee suddenly appeared from the shadows of a porch and said breathlessly, "See, you thought I wouldn't do it. Where's the one cent?"

"That was so easy!"

"Want to back out, huh? Give me the money."

I reluctantly gave my last cent to him.

We both hid in the shadows to wait for the couple to pass. Then we went back to meet Ah Tyim and Ah Won. When Kee saw Ah Tyim, he said, "I did it! Give me one cent!"

While Ah Tyim gave Kee the money, I thought, he really earned that two cents easily. So I said, "Want to bet on me?"

"You?" they laughed.

"Don't laugh. What if I do?"

"I'll bet you one cent," Kee and Ah Tyim both said.

Two cents would buy two feet of sugarcane, so I said, "A promise is a promise."

I hooked Kee and Ah Tyim's fingers, spit on the ground, and we pulled out a strand of hair to seal the bargain.

We walked slowly, waiting for a second couple. Far away we saw the thin, long shadows of another couple. They turned from a different street and walked toward us. I squinted my eyes, trying to focus better. It couldn't be, I thought. I didn't get a chance to look closely, because they turned back.

I challenged, "Hey, you want to bet on that couple?"

"If you have the guts," they said.

"You'll see," I said confidently.

"I'll pretend to chase you," Ah Tyim volunteered.

I did exactly as Kee had done. I ran as fast as I could. Before the couple turned into another street, I caught up. I didn't think of anything—I just ran. I dashed between them and separated them. As I was congratulating myself that I could earn two cents so easily, I heard the girl scream, "*Aiyah!*"

The voice sounded so familiar that I turned to look. "Oh, no," I said to myself. I was petrified.

As I was trying to decide whether I should keep going, I heard the man say, "Is that you, Yeung Ying?"

After pausing a few seconds, I turned into another

block as fast as I could. I didn't care about the two cents. I just ran. I wished I could run to someplace that nobody knew me. Finally Ah Tyim called to me.

"Why don't you stop? You already passed them!"

I didn't want to tell him that it was the most handsome man in the world and I had a secret crush on him. I felt very funny inside. I couldn't tell exactly what the feeling was. It seemed as if something had squeezed my heart lightly, and the feeling hadn't gone away.

"When you broke them up, they turned into another side street," Ah Tyim said.

I still didn't want to talk, until Kee and Ah Won came up. I said quietly to Kee, "It was Mr. Hon and . . ."

"Mr. Hon? Did he see you?"

"He asked if it was me."

"Oh, no!" Kee exclaimed. "Did he sound very angry?"

"I don't know."

"What should we do now?" Ah Won was worried.

"I don't know," Kee said. "I hope he's not mad at you."

"I want to go home," I said.

"Okay," Kee said. We walked home quietly. As we neared the village, Kee had a brainstorm. "I have an idea! You pretend to be sick, so you won't give him a chance to punish you!"

"What if he comes for the annual family visit?" Ah Tyim asked.

"Oh, yes," Kee said, slamming his right fist into his left hand.

"And besides. . ."

"Besides what?"

"Nothing," I said, deciding to keep the secret.

They sympathized with me for having to face Mr. Hon on Monday, but they didn't know how to help me. Kee finally said sympathetically, "Here, I'll give you two cents instead of one cent."

"No, I don't want any," I replied. I didn't think his money could change how I was feeling.

5

Kee was very kind to me because I had to face Mr. Hon on Monday, but he didn't know how to help me avoid being punished. And he didn't know what was bothering me so deeply.

On Monday, the whole time Mr. Hon was giving the mid-term exam reports to us, I kept my head down, afraid to look at him, wondering what punishment he would give me. I was sorry that I hadn't pretended to be sick so I could stay at home, but now it was too late. As I was thinking about it, Ng Shing, the class bully, elbowed me. I looked at him suspiciously.

"Your Mr. Hon is calling your name!"

Shing thought Mr. Hon especially favored me because Mr. Hon punished him whenever he did something bad to me. Shing called me Mr. Hon's pet. I liked the nickname very much. I had secretly hoped Mrs. Yu, who was staying home to take care of her ailing mother, would not return to school. Then Mr. Hon would have to take her place forever. But since last weekend, I changed my mind.

"Are you going to get your report?" Shing elbowed me again.

"Oh. . . ." I awkwardly stood up and walked to the front. I looked at the floor, feeling too embarrassed to look him in the eye.

"Are you sick, Yeung Ying?" Mr. Hon asked as he handed me the report.

"No."

"Good. Well, you did very well, especially in literature. I'm proud of you."

"You flatter me," I replied humbly. I took the report from him with both hands and went back to my seat.

I relaxed a little then, because he seemed to have entirely forgotten what I had done the weekend before.

"Oh, would you please come to the teacher's office after school is over, Yeung Ying?"

Oh no, I thought. He's going to get me after all. I regretted not telling him that I was sick.

Ng Shing chanted, "Congratulations! Congratulations!" He was very happy to see that I was being punished.

School was over. I felt as if I was going to my execution. It was the first time I had to see Mr. Hon in the office. I dragged myself there and bowed before I reluctantly went inside.

There were three rows of big desks. Most of the teachers were sipping tea or grading papers. Only a few who lived in town were ready to leave.

"Sit down," Mr. Hon said, pulling up a stool for me. Never before had any teacher pulled up a stool for me.

I sat down, afraid to look straight at him. He seemed even more handsome and educated with his new brown-framed glasses. I played with the handles of my wicker book bag.

He pushed up his glasses, but didn't say anything for a while. He just rested both his arms on the edge of the desk and smiled mysteriously. Finally he said, as if joking with me, "It was fun that night, wasn't it?"

I kept playing with the handles. I had difficulty swallowing.

Suddenly, he laughed. "You are nervous, aren't you? . . . Don't be nervous. I just want to ask you to do me a favor."

"Are. . . are you going to punish me?"

"Punish you for what?"

"For. . . for that night."

"Oh, no," he chuckled. "I would have done the same thing if I were still your age."

"You would have?" I stared at him and couldn't believe what he had said.

"Yes. I was very naughty when I was little."

Suddenly I felt less frightened of him, as though he

were a regular person. "What do you want me to do?"

He lowered his voice and said, "Well, I am supposed to have a date this evening. But I just got a letter from one of my friends from Canton who is coming to see me tonight. I'll have to change our date to tomorrow evening. Would you please tell Ah So?"

"Okay," I said. I almost couldn't hear myself. I felt something squeezing my heart again.

"Thank you."

"May I go now?" I cleared my throat.

"Sure."

As I was about to go, I caught a glimpse of a black-and-white picture of a girl about my age. It was underneath the thick glass on top of Mr. Hon's desk. The girl was wearing a bead necklace. My mood brightened. I asked timidly, "Who is that girl? She has a beautiful bead necklace."

"She's my youngest sister."

"Oh! Did she get the beads in Canton?"

"Yes."

"There really are beads in Canton!" Thinking about beads, I forgot about the funny feeling in my heart. "Is your family rich?"

He chuckled, "No. Why do you ask that?"

"Because beads are expensive, aren't they?"

"I don't think so. My sister often buys them."

"Do you know how much it costs for a ring?"

"I don't know. Not very much, I would think."

"Really?" That brightened my spirits. I said, as if dreaming, "When I become rich, I will go to Canton to buy beads."

"Well, when you have a chance to go to Canton someday, you will not only buy beads. You will also see a lot of things you haven't seen before."

I remembered Kee telling me about *kwailos* and asked, "Is it true there are *kwailos* in Canton?"

"Yes."

"Will the *kwailos* still be there when I grow up? I want to see them in person when I become rich."

"You don't need to wait until you become rich."

"Yes, I do, because the ticket to Canton costs a fortune! My cousin Kee would tease me for dreaming again."

"Well, it's true that a ticket costs quite a bit. But if you make up your mind, you'll find a way to go. Remember how you worked hard for the camping trip?"

"Oh, yes." Believing I really could go to Canton, I asked, "Is there anything else you want me to do? I want to go home and start looking for some way to make money!" The funny squeezing feeling in my heart had completely disappeared.

"No, that's all. But please don't forget to tell Ah So."

"I won't."

I raced home. Kee and Ah Won were waiting for me right in front of the narrow alley. Kee stopped me by pulling my sleeve. "Ah Mei said you were in detention. How did Mr. Hon punish you?"

Instead of answering his question, I exclaimed, "I'm going to Canton!"

"What? Going to Canton?"

"Yes!"

"When?"

"Soon!"

Kee and Ah Won stood there with their mouths open, watching me race home.

Ever since seeing them on the street, I felt surprised to know that Ah So and Mr. Hon were dating. Nobody in my family had mentioned this. Unfortunately, the person Ah So was dating was the one I had a crush on. That was why I had such a funny feeling in my heart. I also had a strange feeling toward Ah So. But I couldn't describe it, and I felt embarrassed for misbehaving the other night. I was afraid to face her and tried my best to avoid her.

But now I couldn't. I ran straight to the kitchen. She was not there. I went back to the living room and asked Ah Pau and Auntie. Ah Pau was kneeling in front of the worship table. Auntie was smoking her pipe. It was unusually quiet.

"Where is Ah So?" I asked Ah Pau.

"In her room."

So I raced upstairs. Her door was closed. I knocked.

She opened the door. Her eyes were swollen, like she had been crying for a long time. Her bangs and her thick pigtails, shiny from hair oil, were a mess. Feeling uneasy, I reported quickly, "Mr. Hon said he has a friend coming from Canton this evening, and he will see you tomorrow night instead."

As if talking to herself, she mumbled, "The lady came again. We can't see each other anymore." Then she covered her nose and rushed back to her bed.

Seeing Ah So cry like she was heartbroken, I discovered that the funny feelings I had toward her were gone. But I didn't ask her any questions.

I went downstairs and talked to Kee, "Who's that fat lady? How come Ah So cried when the lady was here?"

"How do *I* know? Why don't you just mind your own business!"

About an hour later, while I was reciting poems all by myself in the study, Ah So came in holding an envelope and asked, "Could you do a favor for me?"

"What is it?"

She sniffled and wiped her nose, "Would you please give this letter to Mr. Hon?"

"Now?"

"Yes. It's urgent."

"He is supposed to have a friend visiting him."

"The ferry from Canton hasn't gotten here yet. So he's still free."

"School is out. How can I find him?"

"You can go to the teacher's office to look first. If he's not there, you can go to the back of the dormitory to find him."

"I don't know where his room is."

"His room is at the far end of the men's wing. All you need to do is call up to him. He likes to sit at his desk underneath the window to grade papers."

"What do I do if he's not at the dormitory?"

"Well, just ask another teacher in the office where Mr. Hon is. But don't tell them that you have a letter to give him."

"Why not?"

"Because. This is grown-up's business."

"What if they ask me why I want to see Mr. Hon now?"

Ah So fell into deep thought. Then she said, "Take a book with you. You just tell them that you have some questions you don't understand. Whatever you do, *don't* give the letter to someone to give to him. You have to give it to him *directly*. Do you understand?"

"Yes." I got the letter from her. The characters on the envelope were not as fancy as Mr. Hon's because Ah So had only gone to school for a few years. I inserted the letter inside my literature book.

After I left the village, I ran as fast as I could and went straight to the office. Only a few teachers were there grading papers. I couldn't see Mr. Hon. So I went to the back of the dormitory, which was a long, one-story building. I walked to the end of the building, where dim light shone from a half-open window. I rose up on my toes to knock at the window, and someone opened it. It was him. I held up the book and said loudly, on purpose, "Mr. Hon, I have some questions to ask you."

"Okay, wait a second, and I'll come out."

When Mr. Hon came out and got my book, I whispered, "There is a letter inside from Ah So."

He understood, and he took the letter from the book and read it. I didn't know what the letter was about, but I noticed that Mr. Hon's lips were closed tightly without any smile. I knew it must be bad news. I asked bravely, "What does the letter say?"

He didn't seem to hear me. I couldn't control my curiosity, so I lowered my voice and asked again, "What is happening, Mr. Hon?"

"Oh? Ah So hasn't told you?"

"No. She only said you and she couldn't see each other anymore."

He looked at me for a few seconds, then he put his hands on my shoulders and said, "Well, it's not the right time to tell you now. I hope you understand. Could you take a letter back to Ah So and tell her that everything will be alright?"

"Okay."

Mr. Hon took a fountain pen from his shirt pocket and wrote quickly on the same paper. Then he folded it and put it back inside the book and said, "I really appreciate you running back and forth for us."

When he said "us," my heart felt funny again. I asked him, "Are you going to marry Ah So?"

I secretly crossed my fingers and hoped that he would say no, but instead he said, "Someday, I hope."

"Will. . ." I had a hard time speaking. "Will you still teach us?"

"Why not?"

"So I can still see you."

"We'll be relatives then. You'll be my cousin by marriage!"

"Really?" I was thrilled. I had not thought about that before.

"Yes. In fact, you can even come to Canton to visit us if we ever move back to Canton."

"I can?" All the funny feelings in my heart, all the worry that I might not be able to see Mr. Hon again, suddenly disappeared. I was thrilled and asked, "I hope you and Ah So get married soon so I can go to Canton!"

"Thank you. But," Mr. Hon suddenly became serious again and whispered, "since Ah So and I have a little obstacle to seeing each other, please let it be a secret, okay?"

Even though I was not quite sure what kind of obstacle they were facing, I said very seriously, "I promise I will not tell anybody, not even Kee, or Ah Mei, or Ah Won!"

"I believe you," he said. "You'd better go home now."

I got the book from him and ran all the way home without stopping. When I got home, Uncle was already there. He was home early. He, Ah Pau, and Auntie were talking to each other. But when I came in, they stopped at once, as if they were afraid that I would be a spy! I ran upstairs, where Ah So was waiting for me. She saw me and whispered, asking anxiously, "Did you find Mr. Hon?"

"Yes. Here." I took the letter from the book and handed it to her.

With a shaky hand, she opened it.

I said, "Mr. Hon said everything will be alright." Then I added, "He said I could go to Canton to visit you both after you get married."

A shy smile appeared on her face, and she said gently, "He did?"

6

"Go rinse out your mouth," Ah Pau said after she pulled my loose tooth. She was ready to go to the backyard to throw it onto the roof, so my new molar would grow upright.

"Why don't you wait for the rain to stop and then throw it, Ah Pau?"

"I'd better do it now before I lose it," she said. She got a pointed bamboo hat from the kitchen wall and went to the backyard.

I used the half coconut shell as a dipper to get water from the clay cistern. Just as I finished rinsing out my mouth, Ah Pau came in and declared excitedly, "Your lichee tree is blooming!"

"What?"

"Your lichee tree has begun to bloom!"

"Really! Hey!" I dumped the dipper back into the cistern. Without using a towel to wipe my face, I called from the back courtyard, "Auntie! Ah So! Everybody! Come see my lichee tree!"

Auntie was mending Kee's pants in the living room, Ah So was preparing our lunch, and Kee was playing chess by himself because it was raining. I couldn't wait for them to come. I ran alone to the backyard.

Ah Pau came out and put a small, round-topped bamboo hat on me and complained, "You always run into the rain without a hat. Watch out—you'll get wet and catch a cold."

The lichee tree, with fresh, wet, green leaves, had grown so big that it almost completely covered the backyard.

"Where?" I asked, standing on tiptoes to look for the blooms.

"You see that tiny stuff?" she said.

"That's it?" I was a little disappointed.

She said, "They are flowers. I think in July you'll have lichees."

I almost jumped over the backyard wall. "That means I am rich! I can go to Canton! I can buy a lot of beads! I can see a lot of *kwailos* and . . ."

"Ah! Who can believe your empty talk? How can your dumb tree bear lichees?"

It was Kee, standing behind us at the back door to avoid getting wet.

"What dumb tree? When it does have lichees, I won't even give you *one* to eat!"

"Who wants to eat your dumb lichees!"

Ah So said, "Kee . . ."

Auntie, with a needle and thread stuck in front of her *tong cheong sam*, ordered, "Enough, Kee!" Then she picked off a little white stuff and studied it, saying, "I can't believe it. It seems like she planted it only a few days ago."

"It has been five years," Ah So said. She had a dish-cloth in her hand.

"Five years? That's hard to believe," Auntie said.

"Time flies," Ah Pau agreed. She said, "We'd better go back inside before our clothes get wet."

I reluctantly left the backyard and went into the living room, but I couldn't sit still. I was so excited about my lichee tree. I hadn't been paying much attention to it recently. I put on the bamboo hat and was ready to go out again.

"Where are you going?" Ah Pau asked.

"I want to tell Uncle, Ah Mei, and Ah Won to come see my lichee tree."

"Who cares about seeing your stupid tree?" Kee said.

"Kee!" Auntie shouted.

"You'd better wait until the rain stops," Ah Pau said. "It's easy to catch a cold in that kind of spring rain."

"We are ready to eat lunch now," Ah So said.

So I had to wait until I finished lunch. I was very excited and wanted lunch to be over soon. I helped Ah So bring the wooden rice bucket out to the dining table so we could start lunch quickly.

Finally, lunch was ready, and I greeted everybody quickly. "Ah Pau, eat. Auntie, eat. Ah So, eat. Kee, eat." While I was stuffing the rice into my mouth I said, "Tell me again, Auntie, about the time you bought my lichee tree!"

"Well, it's a long story." Auntie used another pair of chopsticks to pick up a piece of stewed pig stomach. She said, "When you first came to live with us, not long after we moved into this new house, your Ah Pau was afraid you would miss your parents when they left for Hong Kong. She wanted Kee to play with you."

"Yeah, tag-along!" Kee barked.

"But Kee didn't want to play with you all the time, especially when he was with Ah Man. They had a 'Great Men's Club.' They wouldn't let you join, even though you begged them and said you would pretend to be a boy.

"One day, they both pretended to play hide-and-seek with you upstairs. It was your turn to seek. You went into the study to wait for them to hide. Ah Man locked the door from outside while you were still counting, and they sneaked out of the house." Auntie covered her mouth to cough a couple of times.

"Then what else?" I asked.

"Of course you cried very hard. I didn't know what had been going on until I saw how badly they treated you. I took you to the farmers' market and bought you a rice cake. Then a lady selling trees asked me if I would buy the last one from her because her baby was crying from hunger. I asked you if you wanted to plant a lichee tree. Do you know what you said?" She smiled at me.

"What did I say? I forget."

"You said, 'If it will have lichees, I want to plant it. If it will not have lichees, I don't want to plant it.' You were so cute."

Ah So and Ah Pau smiled. Kee only mumbled, "Stupid."

"The lady promised me that it would bear lichees, and she gave me a good bargain because she wanted to go home to feed her baby. I bought it for you and helped you plant it."

"I remember planting it."

"Time flies. That was five years ago. Now you are ten. Do you know what you told me?"

"What?"

"You said when you had lichees, you would sell them at the farmers' market and buy a lichee tree for me to plant, too. But I said by the time your tree bears lichees, Auntie would probably already be gone."

Kee cried out, "Ma!" He sounded sad.

"I know my own problem," Auntie said quietly.

"I don't want you to say that, Ma," Kee said.

"Your cough will be gone soon, Ma," Ah So said.

I was not really sure what kind of problem Auntie had, but she coughed a lot. She was the only one who used her own bowl, her own chopsticks, and her own spoon. She even used a separate pair of chopsticks to serve her food, while the rest of us used one pair of chopsticks to eat with and to serve ourselves. I hated to talk about Auntie's illness. It made me sad. So I changed the subject. Stuffing the rice into my mouth and quickly putting down my chopsticks, I stated, "I've finished! I'm going to tell them the good news!"

"Wait!" Ah Pau stopped me. "Do you want to marry a man who has pockmarks all over his face, huh?"

"Of course not! I will marry a handsome prince later!"

"So, clean the bowl!" Ah Pau demanded. There were still a few grains of rice inside my bowl.

I picked up my bowl and rapidly used my chopsticks to rake the few grains of rice into my mouth. "Okay, I can go now."

Before Ah Pau could make sure the rain had already stopped, I shot up from the seat. Ah Pau seemed to want to make it difficult for me. "Where are your manners?"

"Oh, yes. Eat slowly, everyone," I said without waiting for them to respond. I dashed out to the plaza, which was between two rows of gray brick houses. I ran into Ah Won, who was just coming out of her house.

"Come see my lichee tree, Ah Won! It's blooming."

"Really?"

"Yes! I want Ah Mei to see it, too."

Together we went to Ah Mei's house and asked her to come out.

Ah Mei and Ah Won greeted Ah Pau, Auntie, and Ah So. Then we went straight to our backyard.

"See? See the tiny flower buds? There are as many as

all the dust and sand in the world combined!" I was so proud of my tree.

"Oh, I wish I had planted one," Ah Mei said.

"I'm going to plant one. I'll go and look for a tree in the farmers' market later," Ah Won said.

"If you can't find a lichee tree, I'll give you one lichee to eat. Then you can plant the seed. And I'll give you each a bead after I come back from Canton."

"Are you going to Canton, too?" they both asked.

"Yes. After I sell the lichees, I want to buy beads. I want to see the *kwailos*." I tried my best not to mention anything about Ah So and Mr. Hon getting married.

"*Whaah!*" they said.

Then I went out with them, leaving a lot of wet, muddy footprints in the living room.

"Whoever believes your empty talk is stupid!" I heard Kee mumble. But I didn't pay any attention to him. He was jealous, that was all.

7

My uncle's dry foods grocery store, Kun Hing, was between a carpenter shop and bookstore on Tai Gai. The name of the store meant "working hard for prosperity." As I entered, a strong fragrance of seafood rushed into my nostrils—a mixture of dried shrimp, dried octopus, dried squid, dried scallops, and dried oysters. I couldn't help but keep sniffing, because I was fond of the smell. The dried seafood was stored in big glass jars and displayed on two shelves at the left side of the store.

The wall above the shelves was plastered with red banners carrying slogans such as "Good Business," "Best Wishes," and "Safe Inside and Out." The inexpensive items like dried peanuts, dried red beans, dried green beans, salty duck egg yolks, century eggs, rock candy, brown candy, and rice were in little sacks. Each of them had a price per catty written on a piece of cardboard. Everything was displayed neatly on wooden shelves that took up almost the whole store. A small, clean path about two feet wide went between the merchandise and the counter on the right side against the wall.

It was about two o'clock in the afternoon. The store· wasn't as busy as it was near mealtime. The *fohgei*, Bee, was waiting on a customer. Uncle was concentrating on working an abacus with a Chinese brush still in his hand. The sound of him working with the abacus was rapid and skillful—*dick-dick-duck-duck*.

"Uncle!" I called, gasping for breath. "Do you know what?"

The *dick-dick-duck-duck* stopped. Uncle peered at me over the top of his black-framed reading glasses.

"What? You look very excited!"

"I am! My lichee tree has bloomed! Ah Pau said it will have lichees in July. Can you come to see it?"

Uncle took off his glasses, rubbed his eyes, and said, "That's great! I wish I could come and see it, but I have a lot of bookkeeping I need to catch up on. How about tonight when I come home, okay?"

"Okay."

"What about your lichee tree?" Bee asked. The customer had left. Bee was a slightly built, middle-aged man with thick, bushy eyebrows and dark brown skin. He had been working for my uncle ever since the store was open and was one of the most loyal *fohgeis*. Uncle often helped his *fohgeis* when they had a birth, death, or illness in their family.

After I told Bee about my lichee tree, I asked, "Do you want to see it?"

"Will you treat me to some of your lichees when you harvest them?" he joked.

I had planned to sell as many as possible, so I said, "Just one."

"Just one?"

"Yes. I want to sell all of them so I can go to Canton."

"Go to Canton! *Whaah*! Would you take me with you?"

I didn't answer him. I just laughed. As usual, he got a small handful of dried shrimp from a jar for me. I popped them into my mouth and ran all the way home to my lichee tree.

Ah Pau teased me, saying, "They won't grow any faster, even if you look at them every minute."

"See how many flowers, Ah Pau? Does one tiny thing mean one lichee?"

"Yes."

I tried to count them. Ah Pau laughed. "You might as well try to count the stars in the sky."

She was right. It seemed like much more than a couple of hours since Ah Pau had accidentally discovered them. I knew I would be the richest person in the whole world soon!

The next day, everybody in my class knew that my lichee tree had bloomed. Ah Tee, whose family owned a huge star fruit orchard near Buddhist Hill, asked me,

"Are you going to sleep under your lichee tree?"

"Why?"

"That way you can guard your tree so nobody will steal from it."

"I didn't know that. But what do I sleep on?"

"We always build a shack underneath the tree when the fruit is about to be harvested. We have spent many nights sleeping in the shack."

"I'm going to build myself a shack, too," I told her. I thought about Kee finding scrap boards that the carpenter threw away to make a stool for my Ah Pau's seventy-first birthday present. Kee didn't spend any money on it. So right after school, I went straight to look for Ah Mei.

She said, "I can't play today. My big toe is worse than this morning. Look!"

"*Whaah!* What happened to your toe? What are those black dots for?" Black dots of Chinese ink were marked all over her red, swollen toe.

"Grandma said it is wrapped by a snake's head."

"Where is the snake's head?"

"It's unseen. That's why Grandma dotted the ink to unwrap it and make the snake go away."

"How long will it take before your toe is okay?"

"Grandma said when the snake's head is gone."

I said I was sorry about her toe and left for Ah Won's house.

"Can you help me carry some boards home?" I asked

Ah Won. "I will give you one more lichee and one more bead."

"Where do you want me to carry it from?"

After I explained to her, she agreed. So we both ran toward Tai Gai to the carpenter's shop. There were always a lot of scraps in front of the shop.

"Oh, there are only little pieces." I was very disappointed. I looked through them, but the scraps were not very big.

"What are you going to do now?"

"I don't know," I said. "Maybe I'll go in and ask the owner if he has some boards he doesn't want."

"Okay."

So Ah Won and I went inside. The owner wore a pair of *tong cheong* pants that came just to his knees. He had no shirt on, and the muscles on both his upper arms stuck out like two little hills. He was smoothing a big board with a plane, and a pencil rested on the back of his right ear.

The shop was very messy and smelled of sawdust and pine. There were different lengths and sizes of boards and posts leaning against the walls or stacked on the floor. The floor was covered with scraps, sawdust, and chips. There was no place to walk. So I just stood in front of the shop and called, "Mr. Owner, do you have some boards that you don't want?"

"Oh," he said, startled. He stopped and took a towel that was around his neck and wiped the sweat off his face.

"Are you the niece of Mr. Chan next door?"

"Yes."

"What kind of boards do you want?"

"I just want a couple of boards to build myself a shack," I said. I didn't want to tell anybody else about my lichee tree then.

He looked around his shop, walked to the wall, and found a couple of pieces that had knots in them. They were about a foot wide and several feet long. "You can take these two."

"Oh, thanks!"

He helped us tie them together with a small length of twine and then hoisted them onto our shoulders. Ah Won was in front. I was in back because I was taller. We carefully carried them home.

"Help us, Ah Pau!" Ah Pau was just getting up from underneath my tree. She was holding a spade in her hand.

She dropped the spade and helped us unload the boards. "What are you doing?"

"I'm going to build a shack for myself. I'm planning to sleep here so nobody can steal my lichees!"

"What?" Ah Pau cried. "People only guard their trees when the fruits are ready to be harvested—not while they are just blooming."

"But I still want to make sure."

"Don't be silly! Who's going to steal them? The tree is in our backyard, surrounded with a tall brick wall.

People guard their fruit when they have a huge orchard."

"But I still want to sleep here."

"Can you stand the dung from the chicken coop?" The chicken coop was at the right corner of the backyard, while the storage room was at the left.

"I don't mind. I'm used to it."

"The mosquitos will eat you up."

"I'll put my mosquito net here."

"No, you can't sleep here. You'll catch cold. Besides, I just buried a dead cat next to the roots of your tree."

"Why did you do that?"

"It's the best fertilizer you can get."

"Okay, but I still want to look at my tree."

"Well, I don't care what you do. It's your tree. But you can't sleep here, for sure. And don't just look at the tree and forget your homework and your chores."

"I won't. I have to wait for Kee." I had recently been assigned to *dahm sui*, to carry water home from the river with Kee. It was supposed to be Ah So's job. But not long after the fat lady came, Ah Pau said it was not good for Ah So to appear in public too often because she was an unmarried young lady. Kee and I took her job instead.

Before Ah Pau went back inside, she put the spade into the storage room.

"What are you going to do with the boards now?" Ah Won asked.

"Hmmm, I can just lay them down and make a simple bed."

So Ah Won helped me lay the boards right underneath the tree, where it was bare without any weeds, opposite the side where the cat was buried.

"But the length of the boards is not the same," Ah Won said.

"That's okay. Hey, there are so many different sizes of sunlight circles on my bed!"

"It's neat! I didn't know the sun shining through the leaves could make so many circles!"

"I didn't, either. I am going to lie down on my new bed. Do you want to?"

"Yes."

I moved toward the edge so Ah Won would have room.

It wasn't really wide enough for two people, but it was okay.

The tree shaded most of the sun so it wouldn't shine into our eyes. We just lay there, facing my tree and the sky, but doing nothing. Suddenly, we both jerked up and exclaimed at the same time, "A cicada!"

We raised our heads to look.

"It's coming from the top of that branch!" Ah Won said.

But I couldn't spot it. The cicada seemed to know we were looking for it. After a minute, it was quiet.

"It's gone," I said. But I was not disappointed. I had just discovered that there was a cicada in my tree. "I can catch cicadas and sell them to the drugstore, too!" The *fohgeis* would dry the cicadas in the sun to use for herbal medicine.

"I am so envious of you," Ah Won said.

"You don't need to envy me. You are going to plant a lichee tree yourself."

"I know."

But in my heart, it felt good to have her say that.

After a while, I suggested, "Hey, I have an idea! When you and I harvest our lichees, we can go to Canton together and buy beads and see the *kwailos*!"

"Great! I've always wanted to go to Canton! I want to ride in an automobile."

"Me, too," I said. "But I'll buy beads first, then I'll see some *kwailos*."

To make sure that we kept our promise, Ah Won and I hooked our little fingers three times.

"You know, when I plant my lichee tree, I'll also put some boards underneath it just like you did. I can recite my lessons there and won't need to bother my brother."

"Kee can't complain that I bother him, either."

"And Kee can't bother you. You'll have your own place to study!"

"I can even do my written homework here!"

"How?"

"All I need to do is take a chair for the desk, and I can sit on the board. That way, Kee and I won't always fight over the desk in the study."

"I can hardly wait to plant my own lichee tree."

"Hey, I want to count the flowers on the tree. It seems there are more than before. Do you want to help me count them?"

"Yes."

"Good. You count this branch, and I'll count that one, okay?"

"Okay."

So we both started counting in our heads. To make it easier for us, we pointed with our fingers.

"Oh, I'm sorry. I have to start all over."

"Me, too. It's very easy to mess up."

So we both started all over again.

"What's that noise?" Ah Won asked.

We stared at each other. Ah Won sniffed hard. Suddenly she sprang to her feet crying, "Fire!"

8

We ran through the house to the plaza to see what was going on. A strong burning smell rushed into our nostrils. Ah Tyim was running back and forth at the plaza, beating the bottom of a brass wash pan with a piece of firewood and shouting, "Fire! Fire!"

Children were running, crying, screaming, and calling, "Ma! Ma!"

Mothers and grandmas were calling their children or grandchildren home.

Some grandfathers were looking up at the sky and mumbling to themselves. The whole plaza was in confusion. Even the chickens that usually wandered around the plaza were squawking and running. Ah Tyim's watchdog barked constantly.

"Fire! Fire!"

"Where?"

"Ah Yee's house! Very close! Very close! Fire!" Ah Tyim banged and warned again.

Knowing that we could be in real danger, Ah Won at once cried and rushed back to her house. I also ran home, crying and yelling, "Ah Pau! Ah Pau!"

No answer. I suddenly realized that no one was inside the house. Auntie and Ah So had gone visiting Auntie's sister in a nearby town this morning, and Kee wasn't home. Where was Ah Pau? Fearing for myself, for my Ah Pau, and for our house, I was in a panic. I hastened back outside and ran toward the alley. Ah Mei caught me. She called out loudly, "You'd better stay here, Ying! Don't go!"

"No! I have to find my Ah Pau!" I stopped a second but then ran out of Chan Village to the intersection and called, "Ah Pau! Ah Pau!"

The town was in utter chaos. All the men in the town seemed to be rushing from every direction to Ah Yee's house. Some people banged a big gong, running and shouting, "Fire! Fire!" Many people carried pails full of water. Some pulled homemade carts with buckets of water in them. Others just carried buckets on bamboo poles across their shoulders. Everyone rushed toward the fire.

I ran toward them, without knowing where my Ah Pau was and without knowing where I should go. I tried to fight my way through to look for my Ah Pau. But I was knocked down in a collision with a man whose water splashed all over me. I was so frightened that I didn't care what the man was shouting and cursing about. I just cried and screamed for Ah Pau.

"Ying! Ying! Here, Ying . . ."

"Ah Pau! Ah Pau!" Hearing Ah Pau's voice, I felt safer. I knew Ah Pau was all right. I was able to think more clearly. I managed to stand on my feet and saw Ah Pau about ten feet away. She was fighting her way to me, but the crowd had pushed her and was about to knock her down.

"Ah Pau! Don't try to get here! Just stay where you are!" I yelled, trying to get to where she was. Ah Pau was seventy-two years old. I didn't want her to be hurt. She was the most important person in my life. I would rather get hurt myself. Finally, I reached her. Hurriedly, we battled to the side of the street so we wouldn't be in the way.

I wept, "Where were you, Ah Pau?"

Ah Pau wept, too. "I've been looking for you. I'm glad you are with me now," she said.

"I am scared, Ah Pau." I wept again, but I was not as frightened as I had been before.

I let Ah Pau hold my hand. Together we rushed toward our village using the side of the street. The throng of men trying to put out the fire still filled the street.

Smoke, sparks, and burning debris rose up to the sky at the far end of our village. When we got closer, we saw men getting water from our pond, which was the closest water they could find.

Some grandmas were facing Ah Yee's wooden house and flapping sleeping mats in the air at their own front doors. I began to worry. "Will the fire get to our village, Ah Pau?"

But Ah Pau didn't answer me. As soon as we stepped into our house, she rapidly stripped Kee's bed, which was in the living room, and took the mat. She hastened back to our old house, which was closer to the fire. I followed her, not wanting to be separated again. Flapping the mat in the air toward Ah Yee's house, Ah Pau chanted, "Back! Back! Back to where you belong! Back to where you belong! . . ."

While the grandmas were still flapping the mats, Ah Won's Ma was packing, in case they needed to evacuate. Ah Won also grabbed something and appeared ready to run. She was still crying in panic. Her house was the closest one to the fire.

At that moment I couldn't think of what valuable stuff we had—except my lichee tree. I couldn't take the tree with me, but I wouldn't let the fire destroy my tree. So I ran back to my room, dragged my mat out, faced Ah Yee's house, and flapped the fire back to it.

I didn't know how long I had been swinging my mat, when Uncle, who had gone straight to the rescue effort from work, came home. Kee, Ah Tyim, and Ah Man were with him. They were wet and covered with black soot. Uncle announced at the plaza loudly, "The fire is under control now! We are okay!"

Everybody was relieved. The grandmas at once dropped down and bowed to the ground, thanking the heaven god for sparing them from fire. The relatives who had helped in the rescue crowded together, mumbling something about the fire. Then I noticed the burning smell had diminished.

Many small cousins went out to look. I wanted to go, too, but Ah Pau wouldn't let me. When Uncle walked in, she asked, "How much damage?"

Uncle was exhausted. He sat on the daybed and unbuttoned his filthy, wet *tong cheong sam* and answered, "The bedrooms and part of the living room were burned. Fortunately, it is a single house."

"Did anyone in Ah Yee's family get hurt?" I asked while I offered him a basin of water to wash his face. I was concerned about Ah Yee's father because one of his legs had been crippled ever since he was taken by Ghost Walk.

"It's fortunate that everybody in the family is okay."

"Where are they going to stay now?" I asked.

"I guess they'll have to stay with relatives for a while."

Ah Pau lit up her water pipe and asked as she blew the ashes on the floor, "How could it start so far from the kitchen?"

Uncle shook his head and sighed.

Ah Pau's eyes looked anxious. "You mean?"

Uncle nodded and said quietly, "I knew it."

"What do you mean, Uncle?"

Ah Pau interrupted, "Nothing. Don't mind grown-up's business!"

9

The short, fat lady came back to our house. Ah So retreated at once. I knew Ah Pau and Auntie were unhappy about the visit. But Ah Pau politely added tobacco to her water pipe and wiped the mouthpiece with her hand before she offered it to the fat lady. I didn't like the fat lady, either. I knew something was going on among them, though I didn't know what. Just as the fat lady got the water pipe from Ah Pau, I blurted out, "Why did you come to my house again!"

No one expected me to say that. Ah Pau and Auntie looked at each other, speechless. With her eyes popping out, the fat lady cried, "How dare you!" She turned to Ah Pau. "Why don't you teach your granddaughter some manners?"

I expected Ah Pau to be very upset about my forwardness, but she simply said to me, "Go out and play."

From the way Ah Pau spoke to me, I knew something wasn't right. I had the feeling Ah So was in my room eavesdropping. So, instead of going out to play, I picked up my book bag and pretended I was going to do homework at my tree. When I passed my room, I saw Ah So. She motioned to me not to make any noise and to keep going. But I didn't listen to her. I tiptoed in.

Ah So was ready to say something when we heard the fat lady's voice. Ah So put her ear against the wooden wall and tried to listen. I did the same.

". . . I reported to my master, and he was not pleased."

Auntie started to cough, so we couldn't hear clearly what the lady was saying. After Auntie stopped coughing, the fat lady's voice was audible again. Her voice was a little softer now. "Why are you so ashamed for her to be his concubine? She could wear jade and gold all day and all night long if she wanted. She wouldn't need to do any housework. And she would have her own servant. I'm sure it would be much more comfortable than embroidering all day long." She lowered her voice suddenly, and I had to push my hair away from my ear. I heard her say excitedly, "If she has a son for my master, none of you will need to worry about having food and clothes for the rest of your lives. I just can't understand why you don't jump at this chance!"

"Well, I told you before," Ah Pau tried her best not to show any frustration in her voice. "They were engaged before they were even born, and we have already gotten the bride price for the engagement. That's why we can't accept your master's courtesy. We hope that your master will understand and forgive us."

The fat lady sighed. "I really don't know what to do. You make things hard for me."

We couldn't hear anything but footsteps. She left at once without waiting for Ah Pau and Auntie to say good-bye.

I didn't know what they were doing, so I stuck my head out to see. Auntie was motionless, gazing at the floor. Ah Pau sighed and mumbled something. Then she stood. I shot to my tree before anyone saw me.

That evening, Ah So was preparing supper by herself. She wore a black apron in front of her light grey *tong cheong sam* that fit her slim figure perfectly. With a pair of wooden chopsticks, she was beating egg batter, which just about reached the rim of the big serving bowl. *Wip-wip-wip*. Her chest went up and down as she worked rapidly and rhythmically. The egg batter formed a wave above the edge of the bowl, but it didn't spill. I was always fascinated by the way she beat the batter.

"Can I try it?"

"Be careful. Don't spill it," she said. She gave me the bowl and the chopsticks and went to chop up the pork with a big cleaver. The *chop-chop-chop* sound of the cleaver against the wood almost gave me a headache.

I couldn't beat the egg as forcefully as she did or create the wave above the bowl. I spilled some on the floor. The more I beat it, the more it spilled. Finally I gave up.

"Pretty soon you have to learn how to cook," she said.

"Why?"

"So your future in-laws will not complain."

"I don't need to cook. I'll have a maid to cook for me when I get married." It reminded me of the fat lady. I asked, almost in a whisper, because I was afraid Ah Pau would hear me and be upset, "Who is the fat lady? I don't like her at all."

"She is a matchmaker," she said quietly.

"What do you mean?"

"She is a person who tries to arrange for two people to get married."

"You and Mr. Hon?"

"No," she blushed. "With her master."

"Who is her master? Does he like you, too?"

"Unfortunately," Ah So sighed.

"You are pretty," I said.

"You are flattering me," she replied.

"Yes, you are. Everybody says you are the prettiest one in Chan Village," I complimented her. Like Auntie, Ah So was tall and slim, and her fingers were long and delicate. Her complexion was rosy pink. Even though she stayed home almost all the time, her clothes were the best in our family, and her hair always smelled of camellias because of the hair oil that made her bangs and thick pigtails shiny.

Ah Pau said Ah So needed to dress attractively; that way she could catch a rich husband. I was still a child, and far away from worrying about marriage, so Ah Pau said it didn't matter if my clothes were too small or huge. I didn't mind as long as I could run throughout the whole town freely. It was not surprising to me that there were other people who liked Ah So besides Mr. Hon. "Who is the master she mentioned?"

"Ghost Walk."

"*Ghost Walk!*" I cried. I thought about his pale, mean face. I thought about that time he and his henchmen dragged Ah Yee's father away. I thought about how we were all scared at just the mention of his name. "Why *him*? He has two wives already."

"He wants me to be his number two concubine."

"Number two! How about Mr. Hon? Were you already engaged with Mr. Hon before you were born?"

"*Shush,*" she said, putting her finger to her mouth. "No. Your Ah Pau made it up for an excuse."

"Why did she make it up? Why didn't she just tell the fat lady that you are going to marry Mr. Hon?"

"We can't."

"Why not?"

"You know Ghost Walk is the town bully. You know how mean and how powerful he is."

I did know. Everybody in town knew that Ghost Walk would do bad things to other people if he didn't get whatever he wanted. "But . . . can we tell someone if he is mean to us?"

"Who can we tell?"

"I don't know. But when Ng Shing was mean to me, I told Mr. Hon, and Mr. Hon punished him."

"It's not the same, Ying. Ghost Walk's uncle is this county's magistrate. He protects Ghost Walk, and nobody will say anything. That's why Ghost Walk does whatever he wants and gets whatever he wants."

"That's why everybody is afraid of him?

"Yes."

The rice pot lid was popping up and down. The rice was boiling. Ah So hurriedly lowered the heat by taking some of the firewood out. Then she opened the lid. Steam rushed upward. She moved her head aside to avoid being burned.

After the water dried out in the rice, it looked like a snow-white cake with holes in it. Ah So put a metal plate on top of the rice. Then she poured the egg into the plate and put the lid back on again.

"Who is older, Uncle or Ghost Walk?"

"Uncle."

"Uncle has only one wife. Why does Ghost Walk want so many wives?"

"He doesn't have a son. You know that."

I knew he only had four daughters. "Why does he want a son?"

"Well, he wants his family name to last forever."

"But he has four daughters."

"They can't carry on their family name."

"Why not?"

"Because after they marry, they'll have to change their last names."

"Why does he want his family name to last forever, anyway?"

"Because it's very important to us Chinese."

I still didn't quite understand. I wanted to ask her more, but I heard Ah Pau's footsteps and I quit talking. I wished that Ah So would marry Mr. Hon, not Ghost Walk.

10

A week after I talked with Ah So, I was getting ready for bed. Kee was still up in the study. He had been studying hard because his primary school graduation exam would be held at the beginning of July. Ah So was up in her room.

"Is someone knocking on the door?" Ah Pau asked.

I listened carefully. There was a quiet knock.

"I don't know who would come at this time of day," Auntie said.

"I'll open it," I said. I called out to the courtyard, "Who is it?" Before anybody answered, I opened the door. I saw a small person who had a dark kerchief on her head, like farm ladies wore to keep them warm in winter. The kerchief almost covered the person's face.

"Who are you?" I asked.

The person didn't answer me, but whispered, "Is this Yeung Ying's house?"

"Yes. Who are you?"

"May I come in?"

"Yes, but who *are* you?"

As if afraid someone would spot her, she ignored my question, but hurried in and closed the door behind her, whispering, "I have to see your uncle."

"Who is it?" Auntie carried the kerosene lamp to the courtyard.

"She wants to see Uncle."

"Oh? Come in first."

"I can't stay." But she followed us in. "I have to see her uncle." She took off her kerchief. I recognized her. She was a teenage girl who worked at Ghost Walk's house as a housemaid.

At once, Ah Pau and Auntie's eyes met. Auntie said, "Her uncle is not home yet. I am his woman."

"I have a note for him."

I noticed that Ah Pau looked as if a lot was on her mind.

"You can give it to me."

The girl hesitated. Then she got a piece of paper from underneath her clothes and handed it to Auntie. Hurriedly she said, "I have to go." Before Auntie could thank her, she had already put the kerchief back on and dashed off outside.

I could tell Ah Pau and Auntie were anxious to know what the note was about. So I said, "I can read the note for you."

But Auntie said, "I think we'd better wait for Uncle to read it by himself."

I knew Auntie didn't want me to know what the note was about. Ever since I was promoted to fourth grade, I was the one who read Auntie's letters from her brother to her and wrote letters from Auntie back to him. Uncle was so busy at his store, and Kee hated to sit still to write.

That night, I had a nightmare. But I couldn't really remember what it was about. I was scared. I called, "Ah Pau! Ah Pau!" But Ah Pau didn't answer me as she usually did. I was afraid to open my eyes, so I called out louder. Still there was no answer. I finally peeped over my covers.

It was dark and quiet. Where was the kerosene lamp? Where was Ah Pau? Afraid to be by myself, I jumped up and staggered out of the room to the stairs beside the kitchen door. I called as I groped up the stairs, "Auntie! Ah So!"

No answer! I felt as if I was the only one in the dark house. I thought I had been left behind by my own family. Crying and calling with fear, I fled back downstairs in spite of the dark. Someone opened the kitchen door. "Ah Pau is here," she said, holding up a lamp in her hand.

It really was my Ah Pau, but behind her were several other figures in the kitchen gathered around a cot. I heard someone moan.

I rubbed my eyes. I saw Uncle, Auntie, and Ah So, who was crying. There was Bee, too. They appeared to be doing something. I asked, "What are you all doing, Ah Pau?"

At once, the kerosene lamp in the kitchen went out. The kitchen was dark, but I could still hear moaning. I asked, "What's happening? Who is moaning?"

Ah Pau pushed me gently toward my room and said, "You are dreaming. Go back to bed."

"I'm not dreaming. I'm awake. Who is moaning?"

"You *are* dreaming. I'm taking you back to your bed." She held my hand and went back to my room.

I kept asking her, "What are all of you doing in the kitchen?"

"We are not doing anything. You just had a dream." She parted the mosquito net and pulled the thin quilt on top of me and then stuck the end of the mosquito net underneath the mat.

"I'm going back to sleep, too," she said and closed her own mosquito net. I was still awake, until I heard Ah Pau snoring.

In the morning when I got up, I still remembered what I had seen in the middle of the night. I asked Ah Pau about it. She was sitting on the edge of her bed braiding her long, thin gray hair into a bun. But she warned me, "Don't mention that to anyone. You just had a bad dream. If you don't believe me, you can ask Uncle or Auntie if it really happened."

"I know they won't tell me."

"Okay. I know you don't believe me. I can go to the kitchen with you to see."

I followed her into the kitchen. The cot was not there, and there was no moaning, either. The kitchen was exactly the same as usual.

Ah Pau said, "See, where is the cot?"

"I swear I saw a cot." I scratched my head. "How come I had that kind of dream?"

"We can have all kinds of dreams. Sometimes a dream seems real. You'd better hurry and get ready for school. Kee already left a while ago."

As I picked up my book bag and got ready to go, Ah Pau called and instructed me in low voice, "*Never, never* speak to anybody about your dream. Otherwise, we will get into trouble."

"Why will we get into trouble? It was just a dream."

"Some people won't believe it was a dream and will send someone to investigate."

I shivered. I didn't want anybody to come to my house to investigate, so I said, "I will not tell anybody, not even Ah Mei and Ah Won!"

"That's my good girl!"

11

"Where is Ah So?" I asked as I threw down my book bag. She was always sitting beside the round folding table doing her embroidery. Ah Pau knelt in front of the worship table. It was very unusual for her to do that in late afternoon. Auntie was smoking quietly. They seemed not to hear me.

"Ah So!" I called when I went to the kitchen, but she wasn't there. I even went to the backyard to see if she was looking at my lichee tree. She wasn't there, either.

I ran into Kee in the hallway. "Have you seen Ah So?"

He hesitated for a few seconds and said, "Can't you tell I just came home?"

"She must be out," I said. .

During supper, I didn't see Ah So, either. I asked, "Where is Ah So? I haven't seen her since I came home from school."

Kee looked at Ah Pau and Auntie, but he didn't say a word.

Ah Pau lectured me. "When you eat, just concentrate on eating. A child shouldn't ask too many questions."

"I didn't ask you many questions. I just want to know where Ah So is."

"She is out," Auntie simply said.

"When will she be back?"

This made Ah Pau mad. She stormed, and her gold-and-jade earrings swung wildly, "Didn't I tell you a child shouldn't ask too many questions? You still keep asking and asking! You will get into trouble for your curiosity!"

"I just want to tell her something."

"What do you want to tell her?" Auntie asked.

"I want to tell her that Mr. Hon is sick and didn't teach today."

"Oh," Auntie's and Ah Pau's eyes met. Neither Ah Pau nor Auntie asked me what was wrong with Mr. Hon.

Later that night, Ah Pau said to me, "Get ready for bed. You won't be able to get up tomorrow." Ah Pau was sharp. She noticed that I was stalling and waiting for Ah So, who had never been that late coming home before.

I dared not ask her. But behind Ah Pau's back I asked Auntie, "Where did Ah So go? How come she is not home yet?"

Ah Pau seemed to have ears that could hear sounds miles away. "I told you go to sleep, and I meant it!" she said angrily.

The next day when I came home, Ah So was still nowhere in sight. Was she staying in her room worrying about Mr. Hon, who was sick and couldn't teach? I went to her room to see.

She was not there. As I was ready to leave her room, I noticed that her bedroom seemed to be missing something. I stood there studying it for a few seconds. Then I ran downstairs as fast as I could and yelled, "Ah So has run away! Ah So has run away!"

Auntie raised her head from her water pipe, but didn't show any surprise. Ah Pau stood up, slammed her water pipe down hard on the table, and commanded, "Don't talk nonsense!"

"I'm not talking nonsense! Her pillow, quilt, and all her clothes are gone! No wonder I didn't see her all day yesterday!"

Ah Pau looked restless and avoided answering me. She held her water pipe, trying very hard to light it with a paper stick. But her hand holding the stick was shaking. Before she got the tobacco lit, the paper stick burned out. She blew it several times. Every time she blew the stick, her gold-and-jade earrings jiggled back and forth and created tiny tinkling sounds.

Auntie, trying to be as calm as she could, said, "You'd better do your homework. We'll be ready to eat soon."

It took my attention away from Ah Pau's earrings. I demanded, "No, I won't do my homework unless you tell me where she is!"

Auntie lowered her head to blow the ashes from her water pipe to the floor. Ah Pau finally got her tobacco lit, and started to smoke, *boh-boh-boh.* They both ignored me.

"I know where she is!" I was mad. "She's gone to Canton!"

Auntie and Ah Pau were speechless. Their mouths dropped open, but no words came out. They looked at each other.

I burst out laughing, because I didn't expect them to be so serious over my bluff. "I just guessed!"

Ah Pau said without anger in her voice, "Don't joke with us like that. A good little girl should not joke like that."

"I don't want to be a good little girl! I just don't understand why you won't tell me! But I can ask Uncle when he comes home!"

When Ah Pau said, "Go do your homework!" I threw a temper tantrum.

"No!" I said, storming out to my lichee tree.

That evening, I was making a paper ring covered with different colored dots on it to pretend it was a bead ring. I was waiting for Uncle to come home. When he finally did, I asked him eagerly, "Uncle, where's Ah So?"

Uncle, Ah Pau, and Auntie exchanged looks with each other. Then Uncle tousled my hair and said, "Ready for bed? I'm very busy."

Disappointed and angry over the way Uncle answered me, I exploded. "None of you will tell me, but I know! I know that she is married to somebody, but not to Mr.

Hon! Because Mr. Hon is still sick and cannot teach!"

They were all stunned, but I didn't care. Crying, I tossed the ring away and ran out to my lichee tree and threw myself on the boards. My sudden activity startled the chickens in the coop at the corner of the yard. They made *kok-kok-kok* sounds and shuffled at each other for a while, then they were quiet again. The odor of their dung was much stronger, and the humming sound of mosquitos was much louder than inside. But I didn't care, even if I had to slap myself everywhere to kill the mosquitos.

Later, someone held a kerosene lamp in the dark. I felt a bony hand touch my shoulder. I knew who it was, but I didn't move. Ah Pau said gently, "Mosquitoes are eating you up. It was your bedtime long ago."

I kept lying there. I was still mad at all of them.

She said, "A good girl should not mind grown-up's business. Do you know that?"

I didn't answer her.

She lowered her voice and whispered. I could tell from her voice that she was frightened. "You must never, never mention Ah So's and Mr. Hon's names together. Otherwise we will get into serious trouble."

I remembered what Ah So had told me before about Ghost Walk, and I was terrified. I asked, "What kind of trouble?" I hoped Ghost Walk wouldn't drag Ah So and Mr. Hon away.

"Very serious trouble. You're still young, and I am

afraid you will say something wrong and cause all of us trouble. You must promise me never to mention their names together. Do you promise me?"

I wasn't quite sure what kind of serious trouble she meant. But I promised her. Through the dim kerosene lamp, I saw Ah Pau's wrinkled eyes looking very worried. I didn't want Ah Pau to be worried. I would do anything for my Ah Pau so she wouldn't be worried.

12

I woke up with my stomach growling. I hadn't eaten much the night before because of my temper tantrum. So I went to the kitchen and tried to get some leftover rice.

We didn't usually have breakfast—only two big meals a day, one at lunch and one at supper. The wooden rice bucket was hanging in the middle of the kitchen ceiling to prevent mice from getting into it. I couldn't reach it, so I got a small stool and stood on my tiptoes, stretching my arms as high as I could.

My fingers could barely touch the bottom of the bucket. It had a rope handle hanging from a metal hook on the ceiling. I pushed the bucket up, hoping the rope would slip off the metal hook, which it did. But suddenly, I tipped off balance and dropped it, splattering the rice all over the clay tile floor. The bucket rolled toward the door.

I jumped off the stool and picked it up. Unexpectedly,

I spotted something blue-and-white rolled up behind the door. Curious to see what it was, I forgot about the rice bucket. I picked up the thing and unrolled it. I almost fainted! The night Ah Pau told me I was dreaming flashed into my head at once.

"Oh, no!" I screamed. Crying, I rushed to the living room.

By chance, Ah Pau was still in the living room.

"What happened? What happened?" she asked me.

"He's dead! He's dead!"

"Who's dead!" she cried, embracing me at once.

"He's dead! Mr. Hon is dead! No wonder he didn't come to school!"

"Don't say that." She covered my mouth with her hand and lowered her voice and warned me, "Don't you remember that you are not supposed to mention his name?"

"But he's dead!"

"*Dai gut lai see,*" Ah Pau said. She immediately spit on the floor to counteract what I had said and demanded, "Don't say such unlucky stuff this early in the morning!"

"If you don't believe me, come and see!" I held her hand and led her to the kitchen, where I showed her the blood-stained western-style shirt and blue western trousers that, of all the male teachers at school, only Mr. Hon wore.

"Oh!" Ah Pau cried. I heard her mumble, "I thought

73

Auntie had already gotten rid of these. She must have thought I did."

She grabbed the shirt and trousers quickly and covered them up as if afraid someone would come in and see them.

"Listen," she instructed me very solemnly, "you must *never* mention these clothes. Do you understand?"

I didn't lower my voice, but asked unclearly through my tears, "Why did you say that it was a dream? Why didn't you tell me that Mr. Hon was dead? No wonder Ah So has run away!"

"You said it again. I told you never to mention his name again or to say those unlucky words." She put her mouth to my ear and added, "Especially don't say anything about those clothes. He is in Canton. Ah So is taking care of him because he was beaten up badly."

"Oh!" I smiled suddenly. "He isn't dead?"

"You mentioned that word again."

"I'm sorry. I couldn't help it. Did Ghost Walk beat him up?"

Ah Pau looked at me for a second. She said, "Don't ask me anything more. We are thankful for the help of the young maid and that he's alive."

I knew it was true. I didn't ask her again how bad he was—as long as he was alive, as long as Ah So was not married to somebody else, as long as I still had a chance to visit them in Canton.

"And never repeat what I said to you a while ago about the clothes. Otherwise we'll all be put in jail."

I shivered. "I will not tell anybody, not even Kee, Ah Pau. I don't want all of us to be put in jail."

"Good girl," Ah Pau relaxed. She said, "Here." Ah Pau took one cent out of her *tong cheong sam* pocket. "Get a piece of cooked sweet potato on the way to school."

"I am not hungry anymore, Ah Pau." The news was much better than a full stomach. On my way to school, when I thought about Mr. Hon, I remembered that when Mr. Leung came to take Mr. Hon's place, he acted funny, as if he was hiding something when he told us Mr. Hon was sick. Was he afraid of getting into trouble, too? I didn't know. Now I couldn't tell my friends that Mr. Hon would not come back to teach us. But I was glad that Ah So and Mr. Hon were together, and I still had a chance to visit them after I sold my lichees!

13

When I came home from school a few days later, I asked Auntie, "Are you all right?" Her eyes looked as if she had been crying. But she just shook her head. Then I noticed a teacup on the table—someone had come to visit.

"You can't go upstairs. Go to Ah Mei's house to do your homework," Ah Pau said to me. She looked drained.

"Why not? Has the fat lady been here again?"

Ah Pau suddenly slammed her water pipe on the table and shouted, "Why do you always keep asking 'Why? Why? Why?' When I tell you you can't, that means you can't!"

I was stunned, and tears clouded my eyes. Ah Pau had never yelled at me like that just for asking "Why?"

Ah Pau's sudden action surprised her, too, because at once she embraced me and cried, "Oh, I don't know why I did that! I don't know why I did that. . . ."

Tears began to stream down my face, even though I tried hard not to cry. But it was difficult to do because Ah Pau was crying as well. Finally, Auntie parted us, saying, "Your Ah Pau has a lot of pressure on her, and she didn't mean to yell at you."

Then she comforted Ah Pau by saying, "It's hard for everybody." She offered Ah Pau a cup of hot tea.

After wiping both her tears and mine with the front of her tunic, Ah Pau took a sip of the tea and offered some to me. "You drink some and it will make you feel better, too."

I sniffled and took a sip. I felt much better once I knew Ah Pau didn't really mean to yell at me.

Auntie lowered her voice and said, "Uncle is upstairs discussing something."

With that fat lady? How come Uncle is already home? I had questions, but I dared not ask them. I didn't want Ah Pau to be upset about my questions. I wanted to be a good girl.

Instead of going to Ah Mei's house, I went to the pond and sat on the shore. Nobody was there—only several groups of brown-and-gray ducks swimming in the pond. I didn't feel like helping Ah Pau by calling our ducks home. I didn't feel like admiring the brilliant diamonds that shone on top of the water as I usually did. I just threw some rocks into the water and watched the ripples as they got bigger and bigger, then disappeared. Hearing the rocks *dump-dump* into the water, I felt that I was the only one in the whole, wide world with so many questions—like many threads all tangled up—and no one to help me untangle them.

"Hey, Ying!"

It startled me. Ah Won was carrying a chamber pot and was ready to clean it on the shore, not far from me. Looking scared, she said, "Do you know Ghost Walk is at your house?"

"Ghost Walk?" I felt my heart almost jump out of my mouth. "Why is he at *my* house? Is he going to take my family away?"

"I don't know. Your uncle is with him."

I rushed back to the village. As I turned into the plaza, I tripped on a hen who cried *kok-kok-kok* and flew away. Just at that moment someone was coming out of our house. I didn't see his pale, mean face, but I recognized the stooped shoulders and the ghost walk. I saw Uncle come out, too, behind Ghost Walk, who was taller. But it didn't look like Ghost Walk was dragging Uncle. Instead, Uncle was carrying a big, wooden case with both hands. It seemed heavy for him. Uncle was not built like a laborer, but looked like an educated scholar.

"Where are you going, Uncle?"

He turned without a smile on his face and simply said, "Go home."

I rushed into the house. Ah Pau and Auntie were weeping.

"Did Ghost Walk hurt you?"

Auntie shook her head.

"I am glad. But what did he want? What was Uncle carrying?"

They didn't answer me and kept on crying.

I declared, "If Ghost Walk took advantage of you, I will kick his rear the next time he comes!"

"You will make more trouble for us," Ah Pau said, wiping her nose. "We have trouble enough!"

"What trouble? Did they find out? . . ."

Ah Pau interrupted, "You did it again."

I was silent. I picked up my book bag and left the living room for my tree. As I walked down the hall past my room, I heard Auntie sigh and say, "I don't understand why he never said Kee's grandfather owed his family money before."

Ah Pau said, "That's the way he can get back at us!"

14

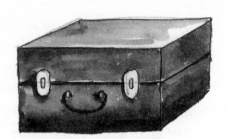

"Hey, look!" I yelled as I ran into the living room a couple days later. "There are tiny lichees coming out!"

Where was everybody? I raised my face up and called out loudly, "Ah Pau! Auntie!"

No answer. They were not upstairs. They must be at the old house, I thought. Recently they liked to go there and seemed to be very busy looking for something. So I ran over to tell them the good news.

The old house, the ancestral home where we stored all our junk in the attic, was next to the narrow alley. We hadn't lived there since we moved to the new house, about five years ago. It was about a hundred years old. The living room was empty except for a long worship table at the end of the room, which displayed all the Chan ancestor tablets.

I pushed open the door. "Ah Pau! Auntie!"

No answer. I walked in, straight to the backyard,

which had no trees but was wild with weeds. I saw that four corners of the yard had been dug up. The dirt still looked wet, and the hoe lay next to one of the corners.

I called out loudly, "Ah Pau!"

"What?" The answer came from the attic, sounding muffled and far away.

"Are you trying to plant a tree or something?" I walked back inside.

"No."

"What are you doing up there?" I heard the sounds of someone moving things around. I had never been up there—it didn't have regular stairs as our new house did, just a wooden ladder made from two small tree trunks with round rungs. I had tried to climb up once but came back down because the ladder felt wobbly.

"We are busy."

"My lichee tree has a whole bunch of lichees now! They look like tiny light green peas."

"What?"

I repeated myself.

"Good!" Ah Pau said. "Now go back outside and don't bother us!"

I was disappointed. "Don't you want to see my lichees? They are all over the tree!"

"I'm not in the mood to see them now. Just leave us alone!" Ah Pau said.

I heard Auntie cough and then say, "Just go back outside and don't bother us now."

Nobody showed any interest in my lichees. As I was ready to leave, I spotted the big wooden case Uncle had carried away with Ghost Walk a couple of days before. It was lying on the corner of the worship table and was unlocked. I couldn't help but quickly open it. *Whaah!* I could hardly believe my eyes! There were a pair of transparent apple-green jade bangles, some gold rings, some gold bangles, some thick gold necklaces, and some gold earrings. They seemed to sparkle! Where did these come from? Is this what Uncle was carrying that day?

"Ready?"

It startled me. Uncle hurriedly walked in. As if I had done something terribly wrong, I quickly closed the case. I didn't know if Uncle had spotted me or not, but my heart suddenly raced.

"Uncle," I greeted him.

I guessed he didn't notice my uneasiness, because he just said, "Uh," to me and raised up his head and called, "Ma!"

"That's all," Ah Pau appeared at the edge of the attic.

I was afraid for her. I called up, "Be careful, Ah Pau!"

"I will," she said. Then she held onto the ladder to get down. I quickly held on to the ladder and tried my best to steady it, watching her climb down cautiously. Her gold-and-jade earrings swung violently when she took each step. After she got down, I held the ladder again to help Auntie climb down. I heard Ah Pau say to Uncle, "That's it. Couldn't find it."

Then I heard Uncle cry, "Why, Ma!"

I turned to look. Ah Pau had taken off her gold-and-jade earrings and was putting them inside the case with the other jewelry. As I saw Ah Pau do that, my mouth dropped open. Uncle said, "Those were your birthday present, Ma."

I had never seen her take them off since she got them from Uncle on her seventy-first birthday last year. I remembered how she admired herself in the mirror. And I was familiar with the tinkling sound of her earrings as she walked. They seemed a part of her. I didn't know why she had to take them off. Luckily Uncle picked the earrings out and said, "Ma, I think you should keep them."

I was glad that Uncle was on my side, but Ah Pau said, "It's okay. I want to do everything we can to keep us from getting in trouble."

I trembled. I thought about Ah Pau warning me before. I thought about Mr. Hon getting beaten up. Were we in trouble now? What did it have to do with Ah Pau's earrings? I held my breath. I was hoping Uncle would insist that Ah Pau keep them. But Uncle put the earrings back inside the case. He looked at them for a few seconds, then closed the case and got ready to leave.

I shouted, "Don't take them away!"

It startled all of them. Auntie by then had stood on her feet. She asked, "What's wrong?"

"Ah Pau's earrings! I don't care what you take, but not Ah Pau's earrings!" I started to cry. Uncle stopped. Auntie embraced me.

Ah Pau also came to me, trying to comfort me by saying, "Ah Pau can buy another pair later."

"Any other earrings won't be the same!"

Uncle turned his head and looked at me. I thought he would change his mind.

Ah Pau said to him, "You go. She'll be okay."

But I was not okay. When Uncle rapidly walked out the door, I tried to run after him. Auntie held me tightly and I couldn't get away from her grip. I went completely wild. Ah Pau had to help Auntie hold me back. I shouted and cried and struggled, "Why do you have to take the earrings? Why do you have to take the earrings?"

Suddenly Auntie loosened her grip and started to cough. Ah Pau shouted, "Look what you have done to Auntie!"

I stopped struggling at once. I became myself again. Then I saw that many of my young cousins were in front of our house, watching for fun. But I didn't care. If they had known what had happened to my Ah Pau's earrings, they probably would not think it was fun at all.

Auntie sat on the floor to catch her breath and coughed. Ah Pau wiped my tears with her hand and sighed, "Even if we don't know if we will have food the next day, at least this will prevent us from getting into trouble."

I didn't say anything, but kept crying quietly.

Then I stood still and let Ah Pau tie my pigtails, which had come loose. After she finished, she held my shoulders and praised me. "See, that's Ah Pau's good little girl."

But I was not her good little girl, because I was still very angry. I was mad at Uncle for taking Ah Pau's earrings away. I was mad at Ah Pau for putting her earrings in the case. I was mad at Auntie for holding me so I couldn't get the earrings back or go with Uncle. If I could have gone with him, I was sure Ghost Walk would be dead from my kicking. I was mad that Kee wasn't home, but was working on his stupid vegetable patch at school. If he had been home, he surely would have helped me get the earrings back. I was mad at myself because I was still a ten-year-old girl, and I couldn't help. I was mad at everybody for keeping secrets from me! So, I went back to our new house and lay under my lichee tree a long time, even through supper, to show them that I was really, really mad.

15

I couldn't stay mad all the time—I wouldn't be able to play if I did. It would drive me crazy. On Sunday afternoon, after I played *yeen ji* with Ah Tyim, Ah Man, and other cousins at the plaza, we began to irritate each other. We were restless because it was already hot in early June.

Kee had also joined in the game. He had been studying hard for his graduation exam. Now he suggested, "Let's go swimming!"

"Yeah!"

Kee, Ah Man, Ah Tyim, and others who knew how to swim ran toward the pond. Ah Won, Ah Ping, and the rest of us who didn't know how to swim raced back to our houses. I went straight to the backyard to the storage room and got a piece of board about two feet wide and six feet long. I carried it clumsily under my arm. Ah Won brought a workbench. Ah Ping and a couple other cousins carried a board similar to mine on their heads or shoulders. Only Ah Wing had a real float. It was made out of seven wooden blocks about seven inches long, three inches wide, and two inches thick, all connected together with two ropes. It was awfully stiff and looked like a giant bullet belt. Not many families had real floats, because they were expensive to buy.

We all ran to the pond. Houses were built along the edge on the other side. They belonged to other families. Over there, wooden outhouses were built on top of the water. Their long foundation poles reflected in the water like skinny, zig-zag legs. By the time I got there, Ah Mei was already there.

"Are you going to swim?"

"No. My toe is better, but the head of the snake hasn't completely gone away yet."

The boys' *tong cheong sams* were scattered everywhere along the shore on the granite rock that extended from Fort Hill. The little boys—Ah Ping, Ah Sum, and others—stripped themselves completely naked. Ah Won and I and the other girls kept our clothes on. We dumped the boards and benches into the water first, then we all jumped in.

"Oh, it feels so good!" I said to Ah Mei, who was about to leave because of her toe. It was the first time in the season we had gone swimming.

We held onto our "floats" and kicked and forgot

everything. We just laughed and screamed. We scared the ducks away to the far end of the pond.

"*Aiyah!*" Ah Won let out a cry when the corner of my board accidently hit her in the back.

"Oh, sorry!" I said as I swam farther away from the shore.

"Hey! I'm the king of the pond! Bow to the king of the pond!" I heard Kee's loud voice.

With my hand I blocked out the sunlight, which was creating thousands of glittering fish scales on the water. I looked toward where the voice was coming from and saw Kee's long, skinny body way up above the water. He was standing on a big rock or something. Ah Tyim was next to Kee, and the water was up to his chest.

Kee was yelling "Bow to the king!"

Ah Tyim and Ah Man each cried, "My turn!"

I held onto the board and swam toward them, yelling, "My turn, too!"

While I was waiting to be the queen of the pond, Ah Mei returned and yelled, "Ying! Kee! Go home and eat!"

"What?" I swam closer to the shore.

She repeated herself.

"This early?" I yelled back because the sun wasn't down yet.

"Yes! Your Ah Pau asked me where you are. Your uncle's home, too."

"Kee, eat!" I shouted to Kee, but I wondered why we were having supper so early and why Uncle was home to eat with us. He, Ah Pau, and Auntie often had their secret talks recently, but he usually went back to the store to eat and stayed until his work was done.

But Kee was having fun being the king of the pond and didn't hear me.

I repeated, "Kee, eat!"

"What? This early?"

"I don't know! Ah Mei said Uncle's home!"

"Oh, oh." The king of the pond was suddenly quiet. He unwillingly stepped down from his throne and swam toward me, asking, "How come *Baba* came home so early?"

"I don't know."

We swam back to the shore and climbed up, letting the water drip from us because we never had towels. Kee used his *tong cheong sam* to wipe himself. His actions were very slow and deliberate. It seemed either he was thinking or he just didn't want to go home because he was having so much fun being the king of the pond.

"We don't have time to dry ourselves," I said. Usually everyone would lie on the granite shore, like a row of dead fish, letting our hair and clothes completely dry in the sun before going home. Sometimes the grown-ups didn't even know that we had been swimming.

Kee didn't respond to me, but slowly put on his *tong cheong sam*. We walked through the wasteland, a half-acre plot of undeveloped land between the village and the pond that was shaded by a huge, old banyan tree. The wasteland was where we dumped our trash, and each family had a big cistern at the back of the wasteland to collect their human waste, which rice farmers would buy for fertilizer. It was like paradise to us. Kee, who was behind me the whole time, whispered, "Hey, go see where *Baba* is."

"Why?"

"Because I don't want him to find out I have been swimming."

"Why? The water ghost will not look for someone now." When I said that, a chill spread through me. The water ghost had gotten my schoolmate, Cripple Yip, a few months earlier. It would look for someone to drown in another three years.

"I know. But he said the water is filthy and full of germs, because we all wash our chamber pots there."

"But he didn't tell *me* not to swim here."

"I forgot to tell you. I didn't think we would start swimming so early this year."

"Will he whip me?"

"I don't think so. You know he is always very lenient with you. Besides that, he didn't tell you himself. It was my fault for forgetting to tell you."

"You just want me to do your dirty work."

"Will you? Just do me one favor."

Even though Kee often bossed me or took advantage of me, he was the closest member of my family besides Ah Pau. I didn't want him to get five licks on his legs with the end of a feather duster. It would leave red marks on his legs for several days. "Just this time," I said.

"Thanks." He was so grateful that he volunteered to help me carry the board the rest of the way.

Just before we turned toward the plaza, he told me, "Go through the backyard in case *Baba* is in the living room."

There were broken bricks scattered at the back of all the houses at the edge of the wasteland. We carefully stepped on the bricks with our bare feet.

"I'll wait for you here," he said when we were just outside our backyard. I went in. The fragrance of food rushed into my nostrils at once. Auntie and Ah Pau were still in the kitchen. I crept into the hall and stole a look at the living room. Uncle was sitting at the round dining table where chopsticks and spoons were already arranged. I quickly retreated to where Kee was.

"You can come in. He is sitting next to the table!"

Kee left the board outside and quickly sneaked in. While Kee was walking though the back courtyard and was about to sneak up the stairs, Uncle came out. Kee was face-to-face with him.

"Oh, no," I moaned while Kee's mouth dropped and he stood frozen.

Uncle looked at Kee a few seconds. "Go change clothes and eat," was all he said to Kee and me.

Poor Kee was like a frightened rooster, still standing there until I pulled him and said, "Go change!"

Neither Kee nor I wondered why Uncle was so

forgiving this time. But I was pleased that Kee didn't get a whipping. Otherwise he wouldn't trust me anymore.

When we changed to our dry clothes and got to the table, I was surprised that there were candles as well as incense lit on the long worship table at the end of the living room. The room was full of the odor of burning candles and incense. I asked, "Is today the first or fifteenth?"

Ah Pau would worship to bless us or give thanks to Buddha on the first and fifteenth day of each month. "Just be quiet and sit down," Ah Pau said.

I sat at my place. Auntie took the lids off the dishes. One was black mushrooms stewed with pork. Another was a cut-up chicken that was still shaped like a chicken, with its head facing Uncle's side and the tail toward me. Another dish was chopped-up chicken intestines, liver, and gizzard, stir-fried with diced cucumbers. There were stewed pig feet, cut in pieces, a dish of cooked lettuce, and a small dish of salty, dried fish.

"Hey, it must be a special day!" I said.

"Shut up!" Kee said quietly. He obviously didn't want Uncle to hear it. He looked serious.

But Auntie didn't say anything. Neither did Ah Pau. I was so happy that the chicken tail was toward me. I hurriedly greeted them, "Ah Pau, eat. Uncle, eat. Auntie, eat. Kee, eat." Then I charged into the chicken tail before Kee got it. I didn't know if it was Kee's turn to eat the tail. He didn't protest, or maybe he couldn't remember, because we hadn't eaten chicken since Chinese New Year.

Ah Pau picked up a piece of chicken thigh, Uncle's favorite, and put it into his bowl. Auntie used another pair of chopsticks to place several big mushrooms and a piece of pig feet into Uncle's bowl. I didn't know why they didn't leave Uncle alone.

I bit into the chicken tail and said, "Ah! It is delicious! I could just eat chicken tail meal after meal!"

I thought they would laugh, but they all remained quiet. Even Kee didn't come back at me. I noticed that Ah Pau and Auntie didn't really eat—they just put a few grains of rice into their mouths. Everyone acted strangely, even Kee. Ah Pau hadn't moved her eyes away from Uncle the whole time! Kee had suddenly turned into a nice cousin. He was unusually quiet as he picked up only cooked lettuce.

I knew something was wrong, but I didn't want to ask. They wouldn't tell me anyway. I just concentrated on picking up one piece of pork, stuffing a mouthful of rice, then a piece of mushroom, a mouthful of rice, and one piece of chicken, a piece of pig feet, until Kee signaled me by kicking me under the table. Then I slowed down and got some salty fish and lettuce.

After I finished my bowl of rice, Ah Pau and Auntie hadn't even finished one-third of theirs. Uncle hadn't finished his, either. I got another bowl of rice, so I would have an excuse to eat more chicken, pig feet, and pork, even though Kee warned me by kicking me again.

Finally, Uncle put his chopsticks down. He had just finished a bowl of rice. Auntie was ready to refill it for him, but he shook his head and said, "I've had enough."

"You will be hungry," Ah Pau said simply. It was her first words since the meal began.

"I've had enough," Uncle said, pushing his black-framed glasses up on his nose.

Ah Pau picked up a small piece of chicken breast and put it into his bowl, saying, "Just eat the chicken. Don't eat more rice if you're full."

"I'm not hungry," he said. But he ate it to please Ah Pau.

"That's good! I can have more to eat!" I exclaimed, hoping to cheer them up. But none of them showed any reaction to what I had said. Kee kicked me again. I gave him a sharp look but kept quiet and ate.

We finished the meal in silence. Ah Pau looked as though she had a lot on her mind. She was restless, as if she couldn't sit down or stand up. Finally she helped Auntie clean the table. So did Kee, which was very unusual. I had eaten too much and was feeling stuffed. I had to lie down on the daybed.

Nobody was in the living room but me. I felt a little lonely, because Uncle also went into the kitchen.

I don't know how long I had been lying there, when someone came in the front door.

"Hey, Uncle Bee!" I greeted him. He wasn't really related to me, but it was the way we addressed someone who was older than us to show respect.

Bee only said, "Ah," and was not as cheerful and talkative as usual. Uncle came out of the kitchen.

"Ready?" I heard Bee ask Uncle quietly.

"Yes," Uncle answered.

They began to walk out. I thought they had to go back to the store again, so I didn't ask why. But Uncle returned from the courtyard and came to me. He lowered his voice and said sadly, "Uncle has to leave you now."

"What do you mean?" I sat up. "You have to go someplace?"

"Don't say that loudly. If someone hears, Uncle can't leave."

"Where are you going? Who's going to take care of the store?" I asked, lowering my voice and playing with the corner of my *tong cheong sam.*

"The store doesn't belong to us anymore."

"Why?" I was shocked.

"I can't tell you now."

"Where will we get money for food?"

"We have to find some other way."

"But why?"

"I can't explain to you now. You'll understand later. I want you to promise me one thing."

I didn't say a word!

"Ah Pau is old, and Auntie's health is not good. You and Kee must help take care of them for Uncle. Okay?"

No wonder Uncle didn't whip Kee! No wonder they had all acted so strangely during the meal. No wonder we had chicken, a farewell meal, to eat this evening. I seemed to understand why he had to leave us, yet I wasn't sure. I didn't want to ask him. I just lowered my head and kept playing with the corner of my tunic to conceal my real feelings. I bit my teeth and tried my best to hold back my tears.

"Okay, I have to go now before it's too late. If anybody asks you where I am, you just tell them you don't know. Okay? Be a good girl." Then he hastily left with Bee.

After they left, I kicked the leg of the table hard, ran into the backyard to my lichee tree, and buried my face in my arms against the tree trunk, letting my tears pour down in the dark.

16

Ah Pau often knelt in front of the worship table and silently asked Buddha to look after Uncle. Auntie smoked even more now and was often in a bad mood. One day when Kee asked her for money for calligraphy paper, she raised her voice and scolded, "Paper, paper, paper! We don't even know if we will have food tomorrow, but all you do is ask for money!"

I knew it was true. When Auntie cooked, she dumped a whole bunch of salt into the cooked lettuce, even into the already salty dried fish. That way we couldn't eat too much. Our clay cistern for rice, with its red banner for New Year saying "Full Always," was not full anymore. It was down to the bottom, and we wouldn't be able to refill it to the top. Before I went to school, Ah Pau said, "I don't have money for your snack, but I hope I will have some soon."

"Where will the money come from?"

"I don't know yet. But I'm sure we will have a turning point."

I didn't quite understand what she meant by turning point. I was a little worried because I was afraid Ah Pau would use the money from my lichees for food. I was desperate not to change my mind about going to Canton.

"I have ways to get money," Ah Pau said.

Ah Pau sold some of our chickens and ducks that were not quite big enough yet—for much less money than usual. Now she only had two chickens and ducks left for Moon Festival and New Year. I was wondering how Ah Pau would find a way to make money.

A few days later I saw a bunch of dried sea grass in the corner of the living room.

"What's that for, Auntie?"

"We are going to weave *sau jau* and try to sell them."

Farmers wore the cylindrical-shaped *sau jau* to protect their wrists while they worked in the rice paddies.

"How do you weave them?"

"I don't know, but your Ah Pau can teach me. She used to weave them before she got married."

Ah Pau came in, holding a couple of wooden objects in her hands.

"What are those, Ah Pau?"

"These are forms for the *sau jau*."

"Auntie said you know how to make them."

"Yes, but it has been a long, long time. I'll have to weave a couple first to see if they are right, and then teach her."

"You can teach me, too."

"Wait until Sunday. I don't want to interfere with your schoolwork."

Auntie had already untied the bunch of dried grass. She and Ah Pau started to pick out the bad straws. I squatted down to help them. Auntie started to cough. Ah Pau looked at her and sighed, "Your cough is getting worse and worse. How can you get well just eating vegetables every day?"

"Don't worry about me," she said after she stopped coughing. "My cough will be okay. After we sell some *sau jau*, we'll have money for food." I was glad Auntie said that.

But Ah Pau said, "It will take a while." She sighed. "I wish the lichees were ripe now so we could sell them. You need more nutrition than just vegetables can give you."

When I heard Ah Pau mention selling my lichees, I asked, "What did you say, Ah Pau?"

Before Ah Pau could answer me, Auntie said, "That's Ying's lichee tree. I don't want to take her lichees. She has a lot of plans. I still have a few nice clothes, and I can get a little money for them."

"She is only a child. She will have a lot of chances later on," Ah Pau said.

I protested, "I won't let you sell my lichees for food! I need the money to go to Canton and buy beads and see things and *kwailos*!"

I was about to cry. Auntie said in a soft tone, "Ah Pau is not going to sell your lichees for food." But then she coughed.

Ah Pau looked at Auntie and sighed, "Your health is more important than her dreams. She is still a child."

"I can help weave *sau jau* for special food for Auntie," I said.

Ah Pau thought for a while and said, "You can learn to do it on Sunday." She moved the grass toward the sunlight. I helped them a little longer. Through the beams of evening sunlight coming into the room, I saw clouds of dust coming from the dried grass. My nose felt itchy, and I started to sneeze.

"Are you feeling cold on this hot day?" Ah Pau asked.

"No," I said. I kept sneezing. I didn't know why.

When I was away from the dried grass, I was alright. Auntie said, "You must be allergic to that grass."

"What do you mean, Auntie?"

"That means perhaps something in the grass does not get along with your body."

"Oh," I said. "Maybe I can make chicken fences like I did before."

"But now it is early June. People who need chicken fences have already bought them at the spring farmers' market. That's why your fences sold so well then."

"How about the *sau jau*?"

"Well, they're different. The rice harvests will be in July and October."

"That means I can't make any chicken fences at all?"

"I am afraid not. Besides that, the fences don't sell for as much as the *sau jau*."

Auntie coughed again. Ah Pau looked at her and sighed.

"Are you crying, Ah Pau?" I woke up in the middle of the night.

Ah Pau didn't answer me as she usually did. She hadn't stopping crying. I slid out of bed and slipped inside her mosquito net. I had never seen Ah Pau cry like that before—not that kind of sad crying.

"Are you sick, Ah Pau?" I asked. I always preferred that I was the one to get sick instead of my Ah Pau.

But Ah Pau cried even harder.

"What's wrong, Ah Pau." I held Ah Pau's hand, just the way she held mine when I was upset. "If you cry, I will cry, too." My nose felt funny, and I started to cry.

When Ah Pau discovered that I was crying, she wiped her tears with her sleeve and said, "Ah Pau is not crying anymore. You shouldn't cry, either."

Seeing that Ah Pau had stopped crying, I wiped my tears with my hand and said, "I am not crying now, Ah Pau. You go back to sleep."

But Ah Pau didn't close her eyes. I could tell from the light of the pea-size flame in the kerosene lamp that hung on the wall.

"Try to close your eyes and go back to sleep, Ah Pau," I said the way she said to me when I had a nightmare.

But Ah Pau couldn't close her eyes. She sighed, "I can't."

"Are you worried because we don't have money for food?"

Ah Pau shook her head on her porcelain pillow and said, "No. I know we are going to make it just eating rice and vegetables."

"So, what are you crying about?"

Ah Pau didn't answer me.

"Do you miss Uncle?"

Ah Pau's tears started to roll down again. She wept, "I don't know where he is, and I don't know if he is safe, and I don't know how to make Auntie stop coughing when she just eats vegetables every meal."

I held her stiff, bony hand and squeezed it. I said, "Don't cry, Ah Pau. I will help you find Uncle."

"You are just a child." Ah Pau cleaned her nose and sighed. "There is a lot of stuff that not even grown-ups can do."

"But we can as long as we make up our minds, Ah Pau. Do you remember I finally got an apple because I made up my mind?" I gently wiped her tears with my fingers.

"That's true. But buying an apple is much simpler than looking for Uncle."

Suddenly, the shiny, glistening beads, the *kwailos*, the buses, the trains, the whole Canton trip was not as attractive as it had been. I wanted to comfort Ah Pau by saying I would have a lot of money pretty soon, but I was afraid that my promise wouldn't come true if I opened my big mouth like I did about the apple. I squeezed Ah Pau's hand again and said quietly in the dark, "I will take you to find Uncle, Ah Pau. I will do anything for you, Ah Pau."

Then I lay down next to her, next to my Ah Pau, and held her hand.

17

Before I started off for school, I went to look at my lichee tree. The lichees were bigger, about the size of marbles, but still green. I wished they could be harvested immediately.

When school was out, I went to the school vegetable garden before I went home. The vegetable garden, which belonged to the fifth and sixth graders, was on both sides of the school entrance. There were small patches of *bok choi*, mustard greens, green onions, and yard-long beans supported by thin bamboo sticks.

As I expected, Kee was there, loosening the soil with a spade. His small *bok choi* plants, which were about three or four inches tall, were skinny and looked sick. They didn't look as strong as the ones next to his. Those belonged to a bigger boy, who was always fertilizing his vegetables. A strong odor of human urine rushed into my nostrils. I covered my nose with my hand while I talked.

"Hey, Kee, why don't you fertilize your plants like that boy does?"

"You can do it if you want to."

"Why should *I* do it. It's *your* garden."

"You eat, too, don't you?"

"You always want me to do the dirty jobs."

"So, don't complain."

"I am not complaining."

"So don't say anything, and leave my stuff alone."

"I'm just telling you the facts."

"I know you didn't come just to tell me that."

I grinned. Kee was very smart.

I squatted down next to him.

When the boy had finished the pot of urine that he was using for fertilizer, he went to refill it. I looked around. There were not many students around, except Ah Man at the corner of the garden. I said, "Ah Pau cried last night."

He looked at me with a question mark in his eyes. His eyes were almost completely covered by his thick hair.

"She misses Uncle." That was the first time I had mentioned Uncle in front of anybody.

"I know," he simply said.

"Do you?"

He didn't answer me, but I knew he did.

"I wish Uncle was home," I said. "She's worried about him, and she's also worried about Auntie's cough."

Kee kept doing his work.

"When Ah Pau was crying, I held her hand. I told her I would help her find Uncle."

Kee swung his head abruptly toward me. "How? You always open your big mouth!"

"I don't mind opening my big mouth to her! She is my Ah Pau!"

"When you open your big mouth, you are just making empty talk. Tell me how, huh?" Oh, the real Kee was back!

"It's not empty talk."

"If it's not empty talk, how can you do it?"

"I can, pretty soon, but I'm not going to tell you now."

"That means you have just admitted that it is empty talk."

I tried hard not to tell him my secret plan—not to tell him that I had changed my mind for Ah Pau's sake. He would sneer at me if my plan for finding Uncle didn't come true.

I said, "I don't care what you say, but I'm not asking you about that. How much money do you have?"

"What? You want to cheat me out of my money?"

"No, Ah Pau only has enough money to buy vegetables and rice, but not any extra to buy beef and liver for Auntie. And I can't help her right now."

Kee didn't say anything, but he worked the soil more slowly.

I grabbed the chance to convince him, "Uncle told me to help him take care of Ah Pau and Auntie. Did he tell you that?"

Kee didn't answer me, but sniffled quietly. He asked, "Do you want to use your money for food?"

"Yes, but I only have a few cents. You have more than I have, I know."

"You are a spy."

I smiled, "Will you?"

"Let me think about it."

"Think! Why do you need to think? You are just plain stingy and selfish!"

That provoked Kee. Then, sniffling hard and pulling his hair back, he said, "Whatever you say!"

I knew it was the end of our bargaining, because every time I argued with him, he often used that phrase when he was about to lose the battle.

"You are stingy! You are selfish!" I stood up and stormed off. I was upset that Kee wouldn't help. I decided to solve the problem by myself, even though I didn't have any idea how. Then I heard Ah Man yell from where he was, "I think we can eat mine in a couple of weeks!"

The next day I waited until Kee came home from school, and I sneaked out of the backyard. Ah Won was sitting by herself on the stone bench next to her house. She asked, "Where are you going?"

"To school."

"Why?"

"I have something to do."

"Can I go with you? I just had a fight with my brother."

"Okay."

We both ran all the way to the vegetable garden.

"Everybody has gone," Ah Won said.

"That's why I waited until now to come," I said.

"Why?"

"I don't want Kee to know I'm here. He said he didn't want me to touch his stuff."

"What are you going to do?"

"I have a plan. Wait and see." I didn't go straight to Kee's patch, but took one clay pot from the corner near Ah Man's patch.

"Are you going to water Kee's *bok choi*?"

"No, I'm going to fertilize it. Do you want to get the urine with me?"

"I guess so."

"Thanks." I held the empty clay pot and walked toward the students' bathrooms. They were built of wood over a pond right next to the garden.

We stopped right in front of boys' bathroom. "Anybody there?" I called out before we entered.

There was no answer.

"I don't know why the school saves the boys' urine and not the girls'," I said.

"Because the girls' urine is dirty," Ah Won said.

"Why? I thought all the urine is supposed to be dirty."

I don't know," Ah Won shrugged her shoulders. "That's what Ma told me."

"I think there is no one inside."

"Wait," Ah Won said. Then she also raised her voice and called, "Anybody there?"

There was no answer, so we walked in. We both held our noses because of the strong odor.

It was the first time I had been inside the boys' bathroom. Instead of rectangular holes that emptied straight into the water as in the girls' bathroom, there were big, clay cisterns in each section—but not much urine left.

"I can help you tilt the cistern so you can scoop the urine out," Ah Won suggested.

"Good idea," I said and found the long-handled dipper in the corner.

Ah Won used both hands to tilt the cistern and held her breath. I used one hand to hold my nose and another to scoop out the urine. I tried to scoop very quickly because Ah Won's cheeks looked like two little drums, and her whole face was turning red. Finally she motioned that she couldn't hold her breath any longer. We both stopped and ran outside to take a breath.

"Oh, my lungs were about to explode!" Ah Won said. The color of her face was returning to normal.

"I'm sorry. When we go back, let me hold the cistern and you scoop the urine so you will have a hand to hold your nose."

"That's okay, I don't mind."

"Ah Won," I said to her, "I like you very much. You don't mind helping with even the most odd jobs."

"I like you, too. You don't like to take advantage of others."

"Thanks for saying that, but sometimes I do, you know." I was embarrassed.

"Well, you've never done it to me."

That made me feel good. "Because you are nice to me, I want to be nice to you, too."

"You are my good friend," Ah Won said.

We both hooked our little fingers before going back to finish our job.

Finally the pot was full of urine. It was heavy. Each of us stretched out one hand as far as we could to carry the pot and held our noses with the other hand as we walked back to the garden.

"Go straight to Kee's patch," I told her.

"Shouldn't you dilute the urine before you fertilize the plants?"

"No. I want to speed up his *bok choi*," I said confidently, even though I hadn't fertilized plants before. "See, the stronger the fertilizer is, the faster and stronger the *bok choi* will grow."

"Oh!" Ah Won said.

Kee had watered his *bok choi*, but the dirt underneath was still dry. He didn't water it well at all. So with both of us holding the pot, we fertilized one row after another.

"I'm glad Kee loosened the dirt yesterday," I said. "Hey, pour it as close to the roots as possible, so they will get all the fertilizer."

After we finished the pot, we went back and got more urine. It took us three trips to finish our job. I wanted the *bok choi* to have more than enough fertilizer.

On the way home, I told Ah Won, "Ah Man said they can eat his *bok choi* in about two weeks. But Kee will beat him because of me. Do you know why I want to speed up the *bok choi*?"

"No."

"So Auntie will be able to eat beef and liver again."

"Why? What's it have to do with the *bok choi*?"

"See, if we have our own *bok choi*, Ah Pau can use the money she spends for vegetables to buy Auntie some meat. Ah! I can imagine how Kee will react when he sees his sick-looking *bok choi* turn into the healthiest plants in just one night!"

"He probably won't believe his own eyes!"

"You're right. Hey, don't tell him we fertilized it. He probably will think it's some kind of magic. Okay?"

"Okay," Ah Won nodded. She was ready to swear, but I said, "I trust you."

She still swore. "I swear. On top of me is the heaven god, below me is the earth god. I am Chan Ah Won, in the middle. If I break my promise, I will be punished by the heaven god and the earth god."

We giggled all the way back to the village.

18

The next day Kee stormed into the backyard. He looked angry enough to kill someone. Without saying anything, he slapped my face hard.

"What are you doing?" I screamed, touching my face.

"Who told you to mess with my stuff!"

"What stuff!"

"My *bok choi!*"

Uh oh, I thought. Ah Won has betrayed me.

"Go look! All my plants are *dead!*"

"All *dead?*"

"*All dead!* Go look! What did you do to my *bok choi* yesterday?"

"I didn't do anything! I just fertilized it."

"*Fertilized* it! Didn't I tell you not to mess with my stuff?"

"I just wanted to speed it up."

Kee stared at me hard and asked, "What do you mean

speed it up? Did you add only a little bit of water?"

I didn't say a word.

"Tell me!"

I still kept my mouth shut.

"Or . . . or you didn't add water *at all*!"

"I just wanted to speed it up."

"You *stupid*!" Kee stormed again. "No wonder it all died! You *stupid*! Why didn't you leave my stuff alone!"

"I just wanted to help," I cried. "I just wanted Auntie to have beef to eat."

"Do you think I didn't want to help? Now you have completely ruined my project *and* my plan!"

"What plan? Why didn't you tell me when I talked to you?"

"Why should I tell *you*! Now you have completely ruined everything, and you don't even say that you're sorry!"

"*Sorry, sorry, sorry!*" I yelled from the bottom of my lungs, but I didn't really mean it. Who would feel sorry toward such a stingy, selfish person anyway?

I stormed out of the backyard while he yelled back, "Don't expect me to give one bite of my *bok choi* to you!"

"Who cares about your dumb *bok choi*!"

I ran into Ah Won in front of our house. She immediately told me, "I didn't say anything! I didn't say anything!"

Switching all my anger from Kee to Ah Won, I screamed, "Traitor!" and ran all the way to the vegetable garden.

* * *

The next day when we bowed to Mrs. Yu, who was wearing a white flower made from yarn because of the death of her mother, she said, "Stand up, Yeung Ying."

I heard Ng Shing make a noise that sounded like he was happy for what would happen next.

I stood up, feeling a little uneasy. Mrs. Yu didn't have a smile on her face, and her voice was flat.

"Did you do it?"

I looked at her, not knowing what she was talking about. At once I sensed that everybody was looking at me.

"I don't understand what you mean, Mrs. Yu," I whispered.

"I mean Chan Kee's vegetables. His science teacher said that you completely ruined his garden. Did you do it?"

"I . . ."

"Don't stall! Yes or no!"

I mumbled, "Yes."

"*Why* did you do it? Did you have a fight with him and want to get back at him?"

"No."

"But *why*? If I find out that you destroyed another's belongings on purpose, you will have to see the principal!"

"I just . . ." I played with my fingers. "I just wanted to speed up the growth of his *bok choi*."

"What do you mean? You didn't dilute the urine at all?"

"I didn't know it would die."

At once, the whole class burst out laughing. I felt like the stupidest person in the world.

Mrs. Yu stood silently for a minute. "I believe you are telling me the truth. I will consider that you didn't do it on purpose, so I will not punish you."

The whole class let out a sigh. But I would have preferred to have Mrs. Yu punish me and for the *bok choi* to have lived. I didn't care as much about Kee's project being ruined as I did about my plan to get Auntie some meat.

Ng Shing and other boys sang after the class,

Dum di di dum,
Dum di di dee,
Fertilized the plants
With plain old pee!

I covered up my ears and pretended not to hear them. But from the bottom of my heart I wished Ah Won had kept her mouth shut. This "song" in my class would continue until another new "song" came up.

"Can you play?" Ah Won asked timidly when I came out of my house later.

"No!"

"I didn't tell on you."

"Liar!" I ignored her and ran away from her to Ah Mei's house. Kee was still mad at me. I didn't have anybody to blame. I was mad at my own stupidity. I didn't have another way to get meat for Auntie, not even with our own pumpkin patch, where Ah Pau had only planted the seeds. I wished Ghost Walk would die, Uncle would return home, Ah Pau wouldn't cry at night, Auntie would have meat, and our home would go back to normal. But Uncle was gone day after day, and I didn't know when he would return. My lichee tree wasn't yet ready to be harvested, even though I watched it constantly.

It was around five in the afternoon. Kee, Ah Man, Ah

19

Mei, Ah Tyim, Ah Won, and I had come to get water from the river. The tide was low. Most of the towns-people had already gotten their water from the river that morning when it was high tide, but we were in school and had to get water at low tide.

The big steamboat, *Happy*, which ran to Canton and other small towns around it, was docked at the ferry landing. Waves hit the boat, making the sound *flip-flip-flip*.

Two coolies, who were chanting *hei-ho, hei-ho* to ease the weight, were carrying a huge wooden crate on their shoulders. A narrow wooden plank extended from the landing to the boat. Inch by inch, they cautiously stepped onto the plank, which sunk in the middle because of the heavy load.

"I hope it won't break," Ah Mei said.

I held my breath—afraid that they would fall into the water along with the crate—until they made it safely on board.

Suddenly, Kee elbowed me. "Don't just look!" he said. We were standing on top of the steps next to the ferry landing, ready for a race that we hadn't tried before.

I turned back from watching the coolies, as did Ah Mei and Ah Won.

"Ready?" Kee commanded.

"Yes!"

"One, two, three—go!"

We all stepped down onto the steps, which were about ten feet wide, into the yellowish water. Kee, Ah Tyim, and Ah Man at once dipped the wooden buckets into the water while the girls who were holding the bamboo poles cheered, "Hurry! Hurry!"

Ah Tyim filled his bucket and got out of the water first. Ah Man cried, "No! You are cheating! The water must be to the rim of the bucket!" So Ah Tyim refilled his bucket and fell behind.

"Hurry!" Kee commanded me to put the bamboo pole into the loop of the rope. But the more anxious I became, the clumsier I got. I started to giggle. Ah Mei and Ah Won heard me, and they started giggling, too. I avoided looking at Ah Won because I was still mad at her for betraying me.

"Stop the nonsense!" Ah Man screamed at his sister. Ah Mei held her laughter. They carried their water and were the first pair up the steps.

I finally put the pole in the loop. As I was squatting

down, ready to hoist the pole onto my shoulder, I spotted a cucumber floating not far away from one of the ferry landing pilings. "Look! A cucumber! Let's get it, Kee!"

"No! Just go!" Kee ordered. Neither Kee nor I checked to see if the rope was in the right position on the pole; we just hoisted it to our shoulders. "Catch up with Ah Man, hurry!"

I walked in the front because I was shorter. But the bucket was very close to me and felt too heavy. I said, "Let's put the bucket down and rearrange it!"

"Just go!" Kee said. With water splashing, we got to the top of the steps and began to race home. Ah Mei and Ah Man were about five feet ahead of us, and Ah Won and Ah Tyim were about to catch up with us.

"Hurry! Get ahead of Ah Man!" Kee shouted. I couldn't slow down even for a second because Kee was pushing me from behind. The water was sloshing violently. I could feel it splashing all over the back of my legs. My shoulder was getting tired.

After about half a mile, when we reached the spot where we always rested, I yelled, "I need a break!"

"No! Ah Tyim will catch up with us! We can catch up with Ah Man soon!"

For the sake of the race, I clenched my teeth and used both hands to hold up the pole and ease the weight on my shoulder. But farmers had laid out their vegetable baskets to attract people on their way to the market. The baskets lined both sides of the street at the intersection outside Chan Village, and crowds of shoppers bustled around.

"We can't get through! They're blocking the way!" I yelled at Kee.

"Ask them to move!"

So I yelled, "Excuse me! Excuse me! Please let us go through!"

But they ignored me, and the bucket felt even heavier. My hands couldn't ease the heavy weight any longer. I yelled from the bottom of my lungs so Kee could hear me, "I need a break!"

"No! Just a minute! We're almost home!"

I felt like my back was about to break—I couldn't stand it one more second. I dropped the pole off my shoulder. Kee wasn't prepared for my sudden action, so the wooden bucket hit the ground hard. Water shot up in the air and started leaking from every crack in the bucket. The shoppers shuffled away, trying to avoid getting wet.

"See what you did! You ruined the bucket! *Stupid!*" Kee was embarrassed because people were watching. He was mad as a hornet, and the bamboo pole was still on his shoulder.

"I *told* you I needed a break, but you wouldn't listen!" I cried, watching the water seep out.

Ah Tyim and Ah Won passed us.

"Hurry! Let's carry the rest of the water back before it all leaks out!" Kee ordered. We put the rope in the right position on the pole and carried it again. By now, the weight on my shoulder was becoming lighter and lighter and there was a snakelike trail of water that followed us home. By the time we got to our courtyard, the water just barely covered the bottom of the bucket.

"See what Ying did, Grandma! She dropped the bucket without giving me any warning!"

"Why did it happen?" asked Ah Pau, who had just finishing cleaning the clay cistern and was ready for us to refill it with fresh water. She stared at us, stunned—a growing puddle appeared around the bucket within a few seconds.

"She ruined the bucket! She has to pay for fixing it!"

"He wouldn't let me have a break. I was very tired, and the bucket was so heavy," I cried.

"Why didn't you let her have a break?"

Kee didn't say a word.

I said, "He wanted to beat Ah Man. We were having a race to see who could get home first!"

Ah Pau turned to Kee. "You know she needs a break on the way home. It's too heavy for her to carry all the way home without a rest."

"You think it's not heavy for me?"

"But you are older than she is, and you are a boy!"

"So what! She needs to eat, too. Doesn't she?"

Ah Pau curled up her fingers and tried to knock Kee's head with the back of her knuckles, but Kee ducked away. Ah Pau scolded him, "You dare to talk back to me?

Next time I'm going to skin you alive!"

That was the end of the race. We used another bucket to carry two more loads of water so there would be enough for a day's use.

After we finished the chore, I ran back to the ferry and looked for the cucumber. The cucumber was nowhere in sight, but I was not disappointed, because I had a brilliant idea.

20

I was glad it was not the day for me to help clean the classroom. I had packed my book bag even before the bell rang.

"Why are you in such a hurry?" Ah Mei whispered when our art teacher, Mrs. Lee, turned her back to us.

"I have something to do. From now on, I'll leave school as soon as possible."

"Why?"

I smiled and whispered back to her, "That is my secret."

The bell rang, but Mrs. Lee seemed to know that I was anxious to leave. She talked and talked. I had one leg outside of the desk, ready.

Finally, Mrs. Lee let us go. I shot out the door.

"Yeung Ying!" Unfortunately, she called me back and asked, "Where are your manners? Aren't you supposed to let the teacher leave the classroom first?"

"I'm sorry," I said, blushing, and retreated to my seat. The whole class *booed* me. I waited for Mrs. Lee to leave before I rushed out again.

I spotted Ah Won right in front of our class.

"Can we play?" poor Ah Won asked. We hadn't played or talked to each other since she had betrayed me.

"No," I said, and kept on running.

"Are you still mad at me?" she asked, running after me.

I didn't say a word.

"I didn't tell on you."

"Oh, right!" I replied sarcastically.

"When Ma asked me that day where I had been, I just said I went to the vegetable garden with you. That's all."

"That's all you said?" I stopped running.

"Yes. I didn't break my oath. If I had, I would already be dead from the lightning this morning."

She was still alive after this morning's severe thunderstorm. And even though Kee had told me never to go to his garden again, he was not as mad as when he had first found out. So I said, "I believe you."

"Oh, good." Her face lit up. "So you can play with me now?"

"No, I can't play."

"Why?"

"I have things to do."

"Can I go with you?"

I thought. If she went, she might get half of what I get,

so I started running again and said, "No, you can't go with me."

"That means you are still mad at me!"

I didn't expect that. I returned and explained, "Look, I ruined Kee's *bok choi*, and I need to find a way to get free vegetables from now on so my Ah Pau can buy meat for Auntie. If I let you go with me, you'll take half away from me."

"No, I won't." She lowered her voice and continued, "I heard *Baba* say he's sorry for your uncle losing his store and having to go away. *Baba* wants to help, but he is afraid. So are other relatives in the village. But I'm not afraid. I'll help you."

I was stunned that Ah Won was the first to mention what happened in front of me. Ah Pau had told me that people, even relatives, were afraid of getting into trouble, afraid Ghost Walk would take revenge if they helped, so they just kept quiet. "You aren't afraid to help me?"

"No. We are good buddies, remember?"

I suddenly felt much smaller than her. I mumbled, "I'm sorry I accused you before I knew what had happened." I raised up my little finger on my right hand. We hooked fingers three times—we were good buddies again.

Ah Won was very happy. She forgot to wipe her tears and asked, "Where are we going now?"

"To the ferry landing," I said. "We have to hurry. It looks like it will rain again."

We took a shortcut to River Front Street and ran to the ferry landing without stopping.

The ferry landing was quiet without the steamboat. It would come every other day. I rolled up my pant legs and went down to the steps and bent down to look.

"What are you looking for?" Ah Won asked.

"A cucumber."

"Why would a cucumber be there?"

"I think the farmers dropped it when they carried cucumbers to the warehouses. But I don't see it now." I came up the steps and saw two farmers carrying produce on their shoulders toward one of the piers about fifty feet away from us. The one in the front had already stepped onto the pier, but the one behind was still on the *sampan*.

"Oh," I held my breath as their bamboo pole went askew. They had loaded their basket high, way above the rim, like a small hill. I hoped they would drop a couple of green papayas.

"Hey! Did you see it! Two just dropped into the water!"

"Let's get them!" I said.

We ran toward the pier. By then the two farmers were already carrying their load toward the warehouse. We cautiously walked on the pier, which was about two feet wide, fifty feet long, and stuck out into the middle of the river. It was made of long skinny boards nailed together. A couple of boards were missing, so it scared us. We could see the yellowish water running rapidly below the pier, like boiling water. For the sake of the papayas, we inched to the end of the pier where the *sampan* was docked. I put my book bag down and lay on my stomach to search for papayas. Ah Won did the same.

"Hey, one is behind that piling!"

"Let me get it!" Ah Pau had warned me never to pick up anything from the water because of the water ghost. A water ghost would use anything as a lure to draw a victim to him. I stretched out my arm. "I can't reach it."

"Let me try," Ah Won said.

"Your arm is shorter than *mine*," I said. So I reached as far as I could, feeling my head filling up with blood. "It is floating further away."

I finally got up, feeling a little dizzy.

"Maybe it will drift closer again," Ah Won said.

"I hope so. Where is the other one?" I asked.

"There it is!"

"Oh, I wish we had a long stick!" I said. The other one was floating at the end of the pier, only a few feet away.

"Hey, the men are coming back," Ah Won warned me.

I heard a cracking sound, and the whole pier shook from the way they walked. One of the men was empty-handed. The other was carrying the bamboo pole on his shoulder.

Ah Won and I stood at the edge of the pier and tried not to get in their way. But the empty-handed one shouted at us, "Go! Go! Go! What are you standing there for?"

Ah Won and I retreated to River Front Street to wait for them to carry a second load.

"I don't think they'll drop anything this time," I said to Ah Won while we watched them carry a half-load of cucumbers.

Ah Won asked, "What are you going to do?"

"Maybe the papaya will drift back to us," I answered. I carefully ran to the end of the pier again. "It's here at one of the pilings!" I was very excited. I lay down and splashed the water to let the papaya drift off the piling.

"Can you get it?" Ah Won carefully came up and lay down next to me.

Just then, we heard thunder, and pretty soon it started to rain. The rain looked like thousands of needles slicing into the river and disappearing.

"We have to go," Ah Won said, raising up her head. She got both our book bags.

"Okay." I stood unwillingly.

Suddenly, Ah Won yelled, "There it is!"

"Where?"

"See?"

A papaya with a little bruise on it drifted about a foot from me. In spite of the rain, the thunder, and the dizziness, I quickly dropped onto my stomach and grabbed it. Holding up the papaya, I declared, "Auntie will have meat to eat tonight! I know they will be very proud of me!"

"Let me see," she said.

"Don't look at it now. Let's find someplace for shelter first."

So both of us carefully ran back to River Front Street. As we ran, I stopped short and exclaimed, "There is half a cucumber floating near the shore!"

"Where?"

"Here! You run. You'll get all wet."

The cucumber was just within my reach. I picked it up and ran under one of the eaves in front of a warehouse where Ah Won was.

"Look—it's beautiful! I want to eat it. I'm hungry! Do you want some?" I was ready to break it into two pieces.

"No, I don't like cucumbers," Ah Won said. She looked at the cucumber and said, "Are you going to eat it raw?"

"Yes. I think it's okay to eat it raw. I'm so hungry!"

"But one end of it is turning yellow. I hope it hasn't been in the water too long."

"That's okay. I can bite the yellow part off. The rest of it is still green." So I ate the cucumber while we were waiting for the rain to stop. It was crispy.

"Oh, where is my papaya?"

"I dried it and put it in your book bag."

"Thanks. Thanks for letting me have the cucumber and the papaya. When my lichees are harvested, I will give you one more to eat, okay? Oh, by the way, I cannot give you a bead, because I am not going to buy beads."

"Oh? What are you planning to buy?"

"I am not going to Canton."

"Why not?"

"I have more important things to do than go to Canton right now. I can go next year. My tree will have lichees again as long as I take care of it."

"Are you planning to use the money from your lichees to buy meat for your auntie?"

"No. My lichees aren't ready yet. Auntie needs to eat meat now. That's why I need to come here every day. If I can find one papaya or cucumber every day, Auntie will have meat to eat, and Ah Pau will not sell my lichees."

"If you are not going to Canton, what are you going to do with your lichee money?"

"When I sell them . . ." Even though Ah Won was my good friend, I didn't think I could tell her the truth, not right now. "Oh, don't ask me now—it is my secret. If I tell you, my secret will not be a secret and my plan will not come true. But I'll tell you later. Okay?"

"Okay."

I ate the cucumber almost to the end where it was yellowish, but I was not willing to just throw it away, because it was still crispy. While Ah Won was looking at the rain, I quickly stuck the rest into my mouth.

"The rain is not as heavy as it was," Ah Won said.

"Let's go home now before it rains hard again."

We got ready to run.

"Wait," I called Ah Won back. "I want to hold the papaya up when we get home. I want Ah Pau to see it first. Hey, I know what she will say."

"What?"

"She will say, 'Where did you get such a nice, big papaya?' I bet she will be so happy that she won't be able to close her mouth!"

21

"Look, Ah Pau!" Near the door, Ah Pau was concentrating on mending the bucket that Kee and I had ruined. If the bucket had belonged to me, I would have thrown it away—we had another one. But Ah Pau insisted that after it was mended, it would be as good as new. "Do you see it, Ah Pau?" I raised my voice to get her attention away from the bucket.

Ah Pau looked up and questioned me, "Where have you been? You look like a drowned rat!"

I didn't answer her, but held the papaya up high and said proudly, "See what I've got!"

"Where did you get that?"

"I found it floating near the pier," I said.

I could see immediately that Ah Pau was not as excited as I was. Perhaps it was not enough for a meal, so I added, "I also found half a cucumber."

"You picked it out of the water?"

"I . . . I didn't get *into* the water," I mumbled.

"What is the difference? Don't you remember your schoolmate who drowned?"

"I didn't get into the water," I mumbled again.

Ah Pau didn't listen to me, but instead asked, "Where is the cucumber?"

"I ate it." I regretted that I had eaten the cucumber. Ah Pau would be happier if I had brought it home.

Unexpectedly, Ah Pau raised her voice and yelled, "Oh! You ate the half a cucumber! What if the person who dropped it had leprosy? What would you do? Huh? You throw that papaya away! I don't want it! I don't want to see it!"

I was shocked at the way Ah Pau yelled at me and disappointed that she wasn't pleased about the papaya. I thought about how I had suffered from dizziness, from the pouring rain, but still tried to get the papaya so Auntie could have meat to eat and Ah Pau could have all the money from the lichees to find Uncle. But she didn't appreciate my efforts at all. Now it was for nothing! Suddenly, my nose felt funny and my eyes got blurry. But I insisted, "The papaya belonged to the farmers who dropped it! They took the rest of them to the warehouse."

"How about the cucumber you ate! Do you know who dropped it, huh?"

I hung my head down. I couldn't answer her. I didn't even know how long it had been in the water, because the end of it had turned yellow.

But Ah Pau kept questioning me. "Tell me!"

"I guess it was also from the farmers."

"You guess!" I didn't know why Ah Pau was being so unreasonable. She screamed, "I don't care *who* dropped it! Anything you find in the water is no good! Throw it away! Now! It makes me sick when I see it!"

With tears in my eyes, and frightened about the half cucumber I had already eaten, I threw the papaya outside of the backyard into the wasteland and ran crying upstairs.

The next day after first period was over, we all ran out for recess. Ah Mei didn't play. She took some old yarn with two incense sticks to knit a scarf on the stone bench at the playground. I didn't play, either. I sat with her and said quietly to her, "Can you go to the hallway? I have a question to ask you."

"What question?"

"A very important question. I don't want anybody else to hear it."

Ah Mei looked around. All the other students had scattered around the playground—either boys playing ball and girls kicking a *yeen ji* or jumping rope. She said, "There is nobody here. What is it?"

I lowered my voice and asked, "Do you know how long it takes to find out if a person has leprosy?"

"What? Who has leprosy?" I didn't expect Ah Mei to raise her voice.

134

"Nobody." My face felt hot suddenly. "I just wondered about it."

"Oh, you scared me to death." She started her work again. "Ma said it takes a hundred days to show up."

"You mean to show up on the face and the hands?" My heart started beating fast.

"Sometimes it does, sometimes it doesn't—especially in women. In the daytime, you can't see it at all. But at night under a light, you can see their faces are red and swollen."

"Are they like the other people who have leprosy and hide in the sugarcane fields, and don't see anybody?"

"Maybe. But some of the women in the daytime are just like any normal person. That's why Ma told me never to get close to a stranger."

"How close?"

"For example, hold their hands, or—"

"Or eat the food that they throw away?"

"Of course not! That's the easiest way to get germs."

I shuddered all over. She noticed and asked, "Do you know somebody who has leprosy?"

"No . . . no . . ."

"If you do, tell me."

"No." I deliberately moved farther away from her.

* * *

Later, at physical education, the space around the playground was still muddy. Our teacher, Mr. Wong, decided to practice marching in the middle of the playground.

We stood in two lines. I was the last one, by myself at the end, because our class had forty-three students.

Mr. Wong blew his whistle. "Count!"

We all stood straight with our hands down. The tallest student turned his head to the right and shouted, "One!"

The second one turned his head to the right and shouted, "Two!"

"Three!"

"Four!"

I stood a little way away from Ping Ping on purpose. She shouted, but I didn't know what number she yelled. My mind was not on the playground. I only knew that she turned her head toward me and shouted.

"Yeung Ying!" Mr. Wong shouted.

My heart suddenly jumped very fast because I didn't have any idea what number I should shout back to him until Ping Ping whispered, "Twenty-two."

I hesitated a second, then responded weakly, "Twenty-two."

Mr. Wong blew the whistle. We all changed from "Attention" to "At Ease."

"Yeung Ying!"

I quickly corrected myself by folding my hands

behind my back instead of holding them straight down.

"All march!" Mr. Wong blew the whistle again, and commanded, "Left face!"

I followed the troop from the end of our line.

"March—one, two, three!"

We marched toward the front, with our knees up high.

"Left, left, left-right-left! Left, left, left-right-left! To the rear, march!"

Ping Ping's head and mine bumped each other's.

"What's the matter, Yeung Ying! Are you deaf!"

I quickly turned around. Now I was more nervous than before because I was the *only* one to lead the whole troop.

"Left, left, left-right-left! Left, left, left-right-left! Turn—turn to the sugarcane field."

Suddenly I heard two sharp whistles and someone commanded, "Stop!"

I stopped. I found that I wasn't in the sugarcane field, but was standing on the playground, away from the troop. They were giggling. Part of the troop had already turned right and left me alone, at the far end.

"Come here, Yeung Ying!"

The giggling died down, for they knew what my punishment would be. But I wasn't afraid. I walked toward Mr. Wong.

"What do you do when you are not concentrating?" Mr. Wong propped both hands on his hips.

"Twist my ear and hold up my leg," I replied at once. Everybody knew that.

"So, do it until class is over!"

I didn't cry. I didn't feel ashamed. I just took a deep breath and twisted my right ear with my right hand and held up my left leg backward with my left hand. I wobbled a little bit, but I steadied myself very easily.

The whole troop was quiet. I was the first girl to be punished that way, but I didn't mind at all. I knew the class would expect me to cry. But I didn't. If they had known that I was going to get leprosy—if they had known that I was going to hide soon—they would know that I'd prefer that kind of punishment, every day and every night, than having to leave my Ah Pau, my family, and hide in the huge sugarcane field like all the others who had leprosy. . . .

22

I was glad that it was Saturday. There was no class in the afternoon. Ah Won was waiting for me. She asked, "Are you going to the ferry?"

"No!" I didn't stop. I didn't want her to get my germs.

She ran after me and asked, "Are you going to buy snails with your Ah Pau today? Grandma and I will go this afternoon. We can all go together."

Every year we had our snail feast at the village. Every family participated. But I didn't care—not only because Ah Pau would not have extra money for snails, but because I didn't want my germs to spread to everybody. I said rudely, "No! Just leave me alone!"

"Are you still mad at me?"

In order for her not to get my germs, I yelled, "Yes! So what!" Then I ran home, not caring whether I hurt her feelings or not.

When I got home, I raced to the backyard to my lichee

tree, threw myself on the boards, and cried.

Then I used my calligraphy brush to draw a hundred small circles on the trunk of my tree. I drew two crosses on the first two circles. In ninety-eight days my face would be all swollen.

I didn't know how long I had been lying there. I heard my stomach growling, but I didn't feel like eating. I didn't feel like doing anything, not even counting my lichees, which appeared a little pink and were now almost as big as Ping-pong balls. Could people get my germs if they ate my lichees? I wasn't even wanting to help Ah Pau find Uncle anymore. Nothing seemed worth caring about now.

"Ying, are you there?" I heard Ah Pau calling me, but I didn't answer her. She walked out and noticed that I was crying and asked, "What's wrong?"

"Nothing!"

"I didn't see you come home. Did you have detention?"

"No!"

"So what's bothering you?"

"Nothing. Go away!"

Ah Pau looked at me for a second, then said, "I have saved your lunch. Let me get it for you."

"I'm not hungry." As I said that, I was afraid that Ah Pau would touch my forehead to see if I had a fever. So I said, "I'll get it myself."

Ah Pau mumbled something and left me alone. I went into the kitchen and chose the worst bowl I could find and a pair of old chopsticks for myself. I stood in the back courtyard to eat. But I could hardly finish a half bowl of rice. I was about to scrape the leftovers into our cat's dish, but suddenly I hesitated. Would our cat get leprosy, too?

Finally I scraped it into the garbage can. I wasn't even afraid that the thunder god would strike me because of wasting food. Then I washed my bowl and chopsticks by myself for the first time. I put them far away from the others so they wouldn't get mixed up.

I went out and lay on the board next to my lichee tree again, staring at the sky, staring at my lichee tree, and waiting for the leprosy to show.

At supper, I took my own utensils and declared, "This is my own bowl and chopsticks. From now on nobody else can use my bowl or chopsticks. And nobody can wash them but me!"

"What? Why are you suddenly acting so strangely?" Ah Pau looked worried.

"I'm not acting strangely."

Kee teased, "Don't just wash yours—wash all of them!"

I ignored him and used a separate pair of chopsticks like Auntie did and put a little bit of dried, salty turnip into my bowl. I stated, "I don't want anyone to get my germs! Everyone should have his own bowl!"

Auntie said, "What kind of germs could we catch from you? You don't cough like me."

"We have been mixing up the bowls for ages. I have

never heard of each person in the family using his own bowl instead of mixing them up," Ah Pau mumbled. "People's ideas are changing now, especially the young people."

"No," Kee said. "She's just weird."

I was quiet, but tried my best to put the rice into my mouth quickly, so I could get away from the table as soon as possible. Then I said, "Eat slowly," and left the table.

As I left, I heard Auntie say to Ah Pau, "I don't know what's wrong with her today."

"Maybe she is lovesick again," Kee added.

At night, I hesitated before going to bed. How I wished that I could sleep next to my lichee tree so my germs wouldn't fly to Ah Pau! I secretly stared in the mirror to see if there were any signs of leprosy which would easily be seen under the light. Ah Pau spotted me and was upset. She said, "You know you are not supposed to look in the mirror after dark!"

I pretended that I didn't hear her. If there was any bad thing that would happen to me, I would rather have that than leprosy.

The next day was Sunday. After I got up, I saw that the bucket Kee and I had ruined was in the back courtyard. It had water in it, but the ground around it was dry. Ah Pau had finally fixed the leak! I should have thanked her for fixing the mess we made, but instead I went to the backyard.

It was a beautiful, fresh morning, with dew still clinging

to the leaves and the clusters of lichees appearing more pink than the day before. Cicadas were already chirping here and there. But I didn't feel like looking for them. I just drew a cross on the third circle. I tried not to touch my lichee tree with my hand. I didn't do my homework; I didn't check Ah Pau's and Auntie's progress in making the *sau jau*; I didn't go to find anybody to play. All I did was lay on the wet board and wait for leprosy to show up on my face and my hands.

"Eat!" Auntie called out.

I didn't answer her, either. I knew that it was very impolite not to answer a grown-up, but I didn't care. She didn't hear me answer her, so she stuck her head out the back door and asked, "Are you sick?"

"No," I replied.

"Let's eat. We have beef this meal. Your Ah Pau sold two pair of her *sau jau* to the store this morning."

Auntie noticed that I was not as excited as I should be. She asked, "Something wrong?"

What should I say? If she had known that I was going to leave her and Ah Pau soon, she would understand why I was not excited about the beef.

I dragged myself up.

We had fresh lettuce, sliced beef steamed with salty turnip, and some dried fish. We were rich again.

Ah Pau moved the dish of beef in front of Auntie. But Auntie said, "We haven't eaten meat for days. I want everybody to eat the same amount." She noticed that I didn't have any reaction and tried to cheer me up. "Did the cat get your tongue, Ying? Be happy for your Ah Pau. She has worked hard for that beef. She even bought mudsnails. We thought we wouldn't have them this year."

I loved the mudsnail feast that was held each year. I could have hugged my Ah Pau if I didn't have leprosy. But I didn't respond to Auntie's comment. I just ate plain rice and refused to get any lettuce broth, which we all got by dipping our spoons into the serving bowl.

Ah Pau asked, "Why do you just eat rice, Ying? Try the beef. It's not that salty. From now on, I hope we don't need to put extra salt into the dishes."

Kee, putting the beef into his mouth, commented, "I know why she looks half dead. In physical education . . ."

"Shut up!" I cried out at once. The rice in my mouth spluttered all over the table.

Ah Pau and Auntie didn't know what caused me to cry so suddenly. "What's wrong? What's wrong?"

I started to choke from crying. Ah Pau at once patted my back.

"Don't touch me!" I jerked away, startling her.

"Why not? Why can't Ah Pau touch you? I'm your Ah Pau. Why can't I touch you?"

"I . . . I have leprosy. It will show up in a hundred days."

"What?" Kee's eyes were about to pop out.

"Who said you have leprosy?" Ah Pau and Auntie asked. They were stunned.

"Ah Pau! Ah Pau said it!"

"*Me*? When did I say such an unlucky thing? When did I say that you had leprosy?"

"You said it because I ate the half a cucumber!"

"What cucumber?" Auntie and Kee didn't know what we were talking about. Ah Pau also looked puzzled.

"The one I found in the water."

"Oh!" Ah Pau burst out laughing. "That just slipped out of my mouth because I didn't want you to go near the pier. I was afraid that you would fall into the water. I just said that to scare you."

"But Ah Mei said one hundred days later the leprosy will show up."

"*Dai gut lai see!*" Ah Pau said "knock on wood" at once.

"You mean that I don't have leprosy?"

"Of course not! Do you think you'd be healthy like you are now if you had it?" Ah Pau relaxed. "I didn't know what was wrong. You almost scared me to death."

I put down the bowl. Without saying anything, I ran back to my lichee tree and crossed out all the circles I had drawn. Then I came back to finish my rice.

"What were you doing?" they asked me. They were really confused.

With delight, I said, "You would all laugh at me if I told you!"

"Weird," Kee said, shaking his head again.

I picked up a piece of beef with my chopsticks and stuck it into my mouth.

A couple of days later, Ah Pau sold two pairs of *sau jau* that Auntie had made. I was very thrilled. So were Ah Pau and Auntie. We were rich again. I didn't need to go to the pier to look for vegetables from then on. All I needed to do was wait for the lichees to be harvested so I could accomplish my secret promise for Ah Pau. Ah Pau still cried at night worrying about Uncle, even though she appeared to be fine when everybody else was around. It was hard to wait.

23

"Kee!" I yelled for Kee to come down from the study. "We are going to start!"

Kee flew down to the kitchen. Ah Pau had already laid out the ingredients: chopped-up hot red peppers, smashed dried black beans, a big piece of smashed ginger root, and a large pile of diced raw garlic.

"Help me hold up the kerosene lamp, Ying," Ah Pau said after she put a couple handfuls of pine straw into the clay stove.

"Okay," I said, trying to hold the lamp up straight, so the flame would not blacken the slender glass shade.

"Hold it close to the middle of the wok," Ah Pau said. She put two or three spoonfuls of peanut oil into the wok. After the oil was hot, Ah Pau quickly dumped all the ingredients into the wok. It made a loud, hissing, sizzling sound. Smoke rose. She rapidly stirred everything.

"Oh, it smells good, Ah Pau!" I took several deep breaths.

Kee sniffed hungrily. He hardly ever went to the kitchen, because he had been told that the kitchen, known as the "lowest room," wasn't for men but for women and servants. "I could eat just the spices alone," he said.

"I know you could," Ah Pau said. "But wait."

While the smoke was still rising from the bottom of the wok, she quickly dumped in the whole bucket of snails, which were each about the size of my thumb. The snails had already been soaked in fresh water for several days so the mud would come out. Kee and I had spent a whole afternoon pinching off their apexes—the tips—with pliers.

The sizzling sound of the beans, pepper, ginger root, and garlic died out at once. But Ah Pau kept the fire going and continued to stir the snails rapidly.

It looked like fun, so I said, "Can I help you, Ah Pau?"

"You can try, but it is heavy." She gave the metal spatula to me and took the kerosene lamp.

"It's heavy! I have to use both hands."

"But quick! Stir that side so they will be even," Ah Pau commanded while she sprinkled some water in the snails and put one more handful of straw into the clay stove.

"Let me do it!" Kee said, grabbing the spatula from my hand. He tried to stir them, but he also hadn't realized how heavy the snails were.

"Make it fast. They need to be turned over quick!"

"I'm trying, Grandma." Kee used both hands to stir them. Several snails flew out of the wok.

"Ha, ha, ha!" I teased him.

Kee was embarrassed. He mumbled, "I'll give the spatula to you, Grandma. I'll help put more pine straw into the stove."

Ah Pau stirred quickly and at the same time said to Kee, "I don't think so, Kee. I have to keep the fire going evenly." Then she put the lid on. Within five minutes, she took the lid off. All of the dark, grayish snails were speckled everywhere with red pepper, black beans, and white garlic. Some of the operculums, the lids that close the opening of the shells, had come off.

"Are they done yet, Ah Pau? Can I try one to see if they taste okay?" I tried to hold the kerosene lamp closer to the wok.

Ah Pau turned her face to me, but didn't stop stirring. She teased me, "I know you don't just want to see if they taste right. You want to eat them, don't you?"

Ah Pau knew me well. She dashed in some salt and pepper, poured in a little bit of cooking wine, and rapidly stirred them several more times. Then she picked up a big one with the spatula and held it out to me saying, "Be careful. It's hot!"

"How about *me*, Grandma!" cried Kee.

"Hold your horses, okay?" She chose one for Kee, who said, "I want one bigger than hers! This one!"

Ah Pau picked up the one Kee pointed to.

I put the whole snail into my mouth and sucked all the juice from the shell first. It was so spicy! Then I took the shell out and held it with the opening toward my mouth and sucked. I had only sucked a couple of times when the whole snail flew into my mouth in one piece! I chewed it hurriedly because it was about to burn my mouth!

"They're good, Ah Pau!" I said.

"Good, Grandma!" said Kee.

"I knew it. That's why I gave one to both of you to try." She put out the fire with a long pair of tongs.

"How did you know, Ah Pau? You didn't even try one to see if the taste is okay."

"Experience!" Ah Pau said proudly. She used two dish-cloths to hold the handles of the wok. Kee groped to the backyard, which was dark, and got the piece of board that I used for swimming. He brought it to the plaza, announcing at the same time, "It's ready!"

I held the lamp to lead the way for Ah Pau and announced to Auntie, "Ready! Come and eat!"

The moon shone bright and round in the sky. Kerosene lamps were scattered around the plaza—almost all the families had started their feasts in front of their houses. The whole village smelled fragrantly of spices and mud snails.

"Come and try ours!" some grandparents and aunts called out loudly to Ah Pau and Auntie from where they were sitting.

"Thanks. We will. Come and try ours, too!" Ah Pau replied, waiting for Kee to put some broken bricks in front of our house before he laid down the board, so she could place the wok on the board. "Put the lamp next to the wok, so everybody can see, Ying."

I did as she told me.

"Go get the stools, too. Be careful, and don't trip."

"Don't start eating yet!" I hurriedly went back inside and brought two stools for Ah Pau and Auntie. When I came back, Kee had already plopped his rear on the ground close to the wok. I settled right next to him. Kee and I were the first ones to dig our hands into the snails, and we started to suck even before Auntie handed us the wires and the washcloths. The whole village resounded with *jer-jer-jer*—the sound of sucking snails.

"*Whaah*! You sucked three already!" I said to Kee, who was sniffling because of the hot spices. I had to suck and chew and swallow as quickly as possible to keep up with him.

"Wipe your fingers on the cloth instead of licking your fingers," Ah Pau said.

"I'm trying to catch up with Kee! He's going to eat all of them!" I said. I didn't even go inside to drink tea. I just blew air out of my mouth to cool the fiery hot taste or fanned my mouth with my hand.

Ah Pau and Auntie were using a small wire to pick the meat out. Auntie said very quietly, "Ah So and her *baba* would sure like to be at this feast."

Ah Pau was quiet for a moment and then said, "The cloud will go away soon and we will see the bright sky again. They will be here for sure next year. Then I will stir three times as much as I did now."

"I hope so," Auntie said as she let out a deep sigh.

Ah Pau looked at Auntie but didn't say anything for a while. Then she slowly put the meat into her mouth.

I wished Kee's actions were as slow as his mother's and Ah Pau's. Ah Pau didn't suck because she was missing a couple of her front teeth. But Kee's sucking of the snails was just like the wind sweeping away the clouds.

I complained, "Look at Kee! There is a big pile of empty shells in front of him already—even more than all three of us put together!"

I started to drop the snails with half of the meat still inside, not using the wire to pick it out.

But Kee caught me and complained, "See what she did, Grandma! She didn't even finish hers and still got another!" He had been keeping his eyes on me all the time, even though he was busy sucking his! From then on, I had to pick the meat out with the wire right in front of his face. It took me a long time. Kee had already swallowed another three!

In order to catch up, I didn't care about manners. I stretched my arm to the other side of the wok to pick up the biggest snail. The meat came out easily. I wished every one was that easy. I chewed. *Ouch! Yuk!* Instead of tasting rubbery meat, I bit down on tiny little shells— my mouth was full of baby snails!

"*Yuk!*" I spit out everything on the board right in front

152

of everybody and wiped my mouth with my hand, complaining, "I thought they did not have babies this time of year, Ah Pau!"

"They can have babies, but not as many. Get another one," Ah Pau said.

Kee was happy that I got a mouthful of baby snails. He laughed. "That's what you get for being so greedy!"

While Auntie frowned at Kee, I said, "Shut up!" and went inside the house to rinse out my mouth.

When I returned, several uncles and grandfathers were moving from table to table to taste the snails. Finally, they all stopped at our place to eat Ah Pau's snails.

I whispered to Ah Pau, "They like yours the best."

Ah Pau showed her missing front teeth as she grinned with pride and whispered back to me, "Of course! I was an expert in stir-frying mudsnails even before I married your *kung kung!*"

Ah Pau was very happy and proud. But Kee and I were not. We were afraid to complain in front of the uncles and grandfathers. But Ah Pau could tell what was bothering us and whispered, "Don't worry. I will buy more. . . . Who's making so much noise?"

Everybody turned their heads toward the dark alley three houses away.

Someone answered, but we couldn't understand what they said.

"What was that?" Auntie asked.

"Don't know."

Later Ah Won, whose table was just next to the alley, came and reported, "It was just some men. They came halfway into the alley and left."

"Who were they?" Auntie asked anxiously.

"Too dark. Couldn't tell."

Auntie turned toward Ah Pau with a frightened look.

24

Ah Pau and Auntie had just finished cleaning up after the mudsnail feast. I was getting ready for bed when someone pounded on the door.

"Who's that?" I asked.

Ah Pau and Auntie just looked at each other with fear on their faces.

Kee threw his mosquito net wide open and got out of bed. "Let me check."

Ah Pau warned, "Make sure who it is before you open the door."

"And take the lamp with you," Auntie reminded him.

Kee got the lamp from Auntie's hand and walked to the courtyard. "Who is it?"

Then he turned his head to the living room as he whispered, "Ghost Walk."

"Ghost Walk!" Ah Pau and I cried.

But Auntie said, "I knew it."

"Should I open it?" Kee's voice was strained with fear.

Auntie looked at Ah Pau. Ah Pau looked at Auntie. I grabbed the broom from behind the door in case I needed a weapon. Auntie finally said, "Open it."

Three shadows approached. Before we could say a word, Ghost Walk roared at Auntie, "Where is your husband hiding? We have to talk with you."

Then Ghost Walk, with his mean face and stooped shoulders, gave the other men a signal. One man grabbed Auntie by the arm. She was surprisingly calm. Even though I was holding the broom, I was no use. I trembled all over.

Kee begged, "Please don't hurt my ma!"

Ah Pau dropped on the floor and knelt in front of Ghost Walk, grabbing his pant leg and pleading, "Please take me. Don't take her, please!"

But Ghost Walk struggled to get his leg free, knocking Ah Pau to the floor.

"Are you all right, Ah Pau!" I screamed. But my legs seemed disconnected from my body, and I couldn't walk.

They were already taking Auntie away. I heard Auntie's broken voice, "I'll be all right. . . . I'll be all right."

"Ma! Ma!" Kee yelled, running after them.

His mother said, "Don't! It will only make things worse!"

Kee stopped chasing them and wiped his tears on his sleeve. I was still trembling like a coward, while Kee helped Ah Pau get up. I hated myself for not being able to prevent Ghost Walk from taking Auntie away. At least

I could have kicked his thin rear or hit him with the broom. I hated Uncle for telling me to take care of Auntie when I couldn't seem to do anything.

Ah Pau wept all night long, waiting for Auntie's return. Auntie didn't return until early the next morning. She was crying, with her hand covering her mouth. Kee and Ah Pau hurriedly helped her inside the house and asked anxiously, "Did they hurt you?"

Auntie shook her head and said. "No. But they kept asking me where Kee's father is and demanded more money." Then she coughed. Ah Pau patted Auntie's back gently and helped her sit down.

"Hurry! Get a cup of hot tea for Auntie!"

I got the tea as fast as I could and with both hands I offered it to Auntie. She took a sip and handed it back to me. Then she blew her nose and said unclearly, "If I had known that a daughter would cause this much trouble, I would rather not have had one."

"Don't talk right now. Just rest. I'm going to get some food for you," Ah Pau said.

"No, I'm not hungry."

"Just try. Even a couple of bites is better than not eating anything." Then Ah Pau hurriedly went to the kitchen.

I was glad that Auntie wasn't injured. So was Kee, who stood next to his mother. But Auntie's face looked like a living corpse. She was pale and there were dark circles beneath her eyes. Auntie leaned her head on the daybed. At first, I thought she was thinking. Then I saw tears rolling down her cheeks. I wanted to comfort her, but I didn't know what to say, so I just sat on the tall stool and watched her. Kee didn't say anything, but stood next to his ma and wiped his eyes.

Ah Pau came out with a bowl of rice. She saw Auntie crying, so she put the bowl and chopsticks on the table and said, "Just eat. There's no use crying. It will only hurt your health."

"How can I eat?" Auntie wiped her tears and blew her nose again. "He kept saying how much Kee's grandfather still owes to his family, with interest."

"Kee's grandfather already paid them back before he died! This is just his revenge because we would not let Ah So be his second concubine!" Ah Pau said.

"He also accused Kee's father of taking all the money and jewelry somewhere else. I told him that was not true. We have already turned everything we had over to him, even our store. He said if . . ."

"Ying, out!" Ah Pau suddenly interrupted what Auntie was saying. "Go to school."

I wanted to find out if they were going to send someone to catch Uncle, but I didn't want to upset Auntie and Ah Pau anymore. So I left, even though I felt it was unfair that Kee could stay.

But I was glad that Auntie was home and unhurt.

25

Kee spent more time at home around his mother. She cried often and smoked more than before. She also asked Ah Pau, "How many days left?" over and over.

Finally Ah Pau, who had been working hard since Auntie didn't have the energy to make *sau jau*, said, "I still don't believe it."

"What are you talking about?" I asked. "Why do you always ask that same question, Auntie?"

Ah Pau said, "How many times have I told you a little child shouldn't ask about grown-up's business, huh?"

I pouted and went back to my lichee tree. Seeing the clusters of lichees getting riper each day, hanging heavily on the branches, I didn't pout anymore. I wanted to pick one to try, but I finally convinced myself not to. I thought, I had better wait to eat the ones I couldn't sell because I wanted to sell as many of them as possible.

That way Ah Pau could have a better chance of finding Uncle.

Later, Ah Pau came to feed the chickens. I said, "Can I pick the lichees tomorrow?"

"Why don't you just leave them alone and concentrate on schoolwork!" Ah Pau's voice sounded irritated. Something seemed to be on her mind ever since Auntie had been taken away.

Kee came in and discovered that I was lying down on the board looking at my lichee tree again. "Don't be so excited about your lichees," he said. "You won't even have . . ." He stopped suddenly when Ah Pau looked at him sharply.

It was a strange and powerful look. Wondering why Ah Pau had stopped him, I asked Kee, "I won't even have what?"

Before Kee could say anything, Ah Pau replied, "Never mind. He's just teasing you."

But I thought Kee was *not* just teasing me. He was jealous because he didn't have a lichee tree—that's all!

Two days later, Ah Pau was smoking quietly when I got up in the morning. It was very unusual for her. There wasn't any sea grass on the floor, and she hadn't started working on the *sau jau* yet.

"What's the noise upstairs? Is Auntie rearranging the furniture?"

Ah Pau didn't say a word. She seemed distracted in her silence. I asked her, "Is something wrong, Ah Pau?"

She didn't hear me. I repeated my question.

"Go to school," she simply said.

I knew something was bothering her, but I didn't want to annoy her. When I handed her the money I got from the lichees, she would be okay. She must be thinking about Uncle. So, before I went to school, I looked at my lichees again. I said quietly to my lichees, "I hope you can make a lot of money so my Ah Pau can find Uncle. Please. I promise I will take very good care of you from now on. I will water you more often and I will also try to find another dead cat to bury next to you, because you are my only hope. I don't want my Ah Pau to cry at night again. She is the most important person in the whole wide world to me. Please, please, please." I felt very satisfied because my lichee tree was fresh and content, and it seemed to listen to what I was whispering.

Ah Won looked for me while I was on the school playground. We were friends again since I didn't have leprosy. She asked, "Did you see that Hing Kee is selling lichees this morning?

"No. How do you know?"

"I went by Tai Gai on my way to school this morning."

"Do you know how much he is charging for a catty?"

"I didn't really look. That's why I came here—to see if you wanted to go look when school is out."

"Of course, I want to see!"

When school was out, instead of going straight home, we went to Tai Gai first. On the way there I said, "I am very excited. I hope I can pick my lichees and sell them today. I want to surprise Ah Pau when I give her the money."

At a distance we could already see the red lichees piled up in two baskets in front of Hing Kee. We went closer.

"*Whaah!* Twenty-four cents for a catty!" I exclaimed.

"Oh, yes! The other pile is twenty. I wonder what's the difference?"

"The twenty-four-cent ones look bigger, and they all have leaves and stems on them," I said.

By that time, a couple of people were gathering there to buy lichees. The bald-headed owner was busy weighing the fruits and making change for his customers.

"Look! He weighed the lichees with the leaves and stems on. No wonder there are not many lichees in a catty!" Ah Won pointed out.

"That's good! That means I can sell more catties!"

Pretty soon the customers left. The owner straightened up the lichees. He took a sign that had twenty cents written on it and replaced the twenty-four cent sign to easily sell the leftovers.

The owner finally had time to drink the whole cup of tea beside him. I had bought an apple from him once. He sat on his stool and took his money out of a big canvas bag hanging around his waist and started to count it.

"I will count my money exactly as he is doing when I sell my lichees," I said to Ah Won. Before Ah Won could say anything, I suddenly had a brainstorm. "Let me ask him!"

"What are you going to ask him?"

I didn't answer but walked closer to the owner. After waiting for him to finish counting, I asked, "Would you like to buy my lichees?"

"How do you have lichees to sell to me?"

"I have my own lichee tree. I planted it when I was five. My auntie bought it for me."

"Well, about how many catties do you have?"

"I don't know. But you won't believe me if I tell you. There are as many as the stars in the sky. I couldn't even count them all!"

He laughed.

"I'm not telling a lie. You can ask her."

"Yes. It's full of lichees," Ah Won said. She looked like she couldn't stand still.

"You can come to my house to see it."

"Are they completely ripe yet?" he asked me.

"They are just like the opera actress's make-up!"

"Oh, young lady!" the owner laughed. I didn't know what he was laughing at. "I think you can tell a very interesting story."

"You flatter me. But do you want to buy my lichees?"

"Well, I have to see your lichees first. Then I can decide whether to buy them or not."

"You mean come to my house to see?"

"Of course not. I couldn't leave my store. Why don't you pick up a bunch to show me first. Then I can make my decision."

Ah Won suddenly interrupted me. "I need to pee," she whispered. "I'll wait for you at the alley."

"Okay. Please don't tell anybody. I want to surprise my Ah Pau."

"I won't."

After Ah Won left, I said to the owner, "That means you are willing to see my lichees?"

"Yes."

"A promise is a promise!" I was thrilled and took my hand out to hook my little finger with him.

"Oh, I'm too old for that."

"How can I believe you?"

He hesitated a second, then smiled. "Okay. I think I would like to become a child once again." He put his right hand out, and we hooked fingers three times. Then I pulled out a hair and threw it into the air. His eyes opened wider, and he exclaimed, "I don't have much hair left!"

I giggled.

"You still have to pull it. Otherwise it will not count!"

"All right," he pulled out a hair. His face wrinkled up, showing that it really hurt.

"Throw it into the air," I said. "And one more thing," I instructed. "Spit on the ground."

"Oh, I can't do that."

"Why not? It's part of the promise. See, mine has already dried before you could blink your eyes!"

Finally, he spit. I clapped and said happily, "Now wait for me. I'm going home to pick some lichees."

I was even happier and prouder than the time I presented an apple to my Ah Pau the year before.

26

I started running. Halfway home Ah Won ran back to meet me. She looked like she couldn't catch her breath and was about to cry.

"Are . . . are you all right?" I caught my breath.

She stuttered and pulled me backward, away from Chan Village. "Don't . . ."

"What are you doing?"

"Don't go there. Please don't go there."

"What are you talking about, Ah Won!"

"Please, we can go wherever you want, but not . . ."

"I don't understand you, Ah Won!" I was confused.

"I don't care if you understand me or not. But please don't go home."

"Why not? I need to pick a bunch of my lichees!"

"I . . . please don't. We can go to Buddhist Hill to catch cicadas."

"What's wrong with you? You know I have cicadas on my lichee tree!"

"We can do whatever you want! We can even go to hunt beads under the stage again, but not . . ."

"Didn't you swear that you would never go to that rotten place again? If you don't want to pick lichees with me, just say it!"

"I . . ." Suddenly she cried.

"Okay. That's up to you. I thought you were my good friend and you were willing to help, but . . ."

She started to pull my arm again and begged, "Please don't go. Please don't go."

I jerked away from her. I was mad and disappointed. "Leave me alone!" I yelled.

She tried very hard to pull me back. But she was not as strong as me, so I quickly got away from her and ran toward the alley while she was still calling me not to go. I didn't know why Ah Won was acting so strangely.

As I entered the narrow alley, someone stopped me. It was Kee. I was so excited about showing the man my lichees, I burst out, "Hey Kee! Guess what! I am going to . . ."

"Where have you been? Grandma wants you."

"Why?"

"Just go."

"I am busy. Let me go."

"Are you going?"

"No! Wait 'til I come back."

"Now! She needs you!"

"Is she sick?" I remembered how Au Pau had been this morning.

"You go look. She is in the old house." Kee looked serious.

"Why is she in the old house?" This time I didn't wait for Kee's answer. His seriousness bothered me. I ran to our old house.

As I was about to call for Ah Pau, I noticed a few pieces of furniture from the new house scattered around the living room. Before I could ask what was going on, I spotted Ah Pau leaning on the daybed. She looked ill. She seemed not to see me at all. She didn't say a word and didn't move. I suddenly noticed that her thin hair was all white now instead of salt-and-pepper. Without the gold-and-jade earrings, her ears looked very lonely.

At that moment, I forgot all about my lichees and what I was supposed to do. I just wanted to cry, but I didn't. I tried my best to hold back my tears. As I walked toward her I said, "When I get the money from selling the lichees, I'm going to buy you another pair of earrings, Ah Pau."

What I said didn't interest Ah Pau. She just looked at me, trying to say something. But nothing came out. Tears started rolling down her cheeks. I threw down my book bag and ran to her. "Ah Pau, are you sick? Please don't cry. When I get the money from my lichees, I will take you to find Uncle. I will take you to see the doctor."

That made it even worse. It also made Auntie, who was sitting next to the daybed, start to cry. Even Kee sniffled. I didn't know what was going on. Didn't they like me to care about them? Seeing all of them cry, I couldn't hold my tears any longer.

Finally, Ah Pau wiped her tears and blew her nose. She held me close and said, "Don't cry. Ah Pau is not crying now." Then Ah Pau put her bony hands on my shoulders and said, "Ah Pau wants you to promise her one thing."

"What is it?" I sniffed. Seeing Ah Pau had stopped crying, I felt better. "Oh, I know. 'Don't eat too many lichees. You'll get sick.' Is that it?"

Ah Pau's tears came down again, but she wiped them quickly and said, "Forget the lichees. You have to promise me to be a good girl."

"I *am* a good girl. I didn't even pick one for myself. I want to sell as many as I can for you, Ah Pau."

Ah Pau suddenly covered her face and started crying again. I asked disappointedly, "Don't you like my lichees, Ah Pau?"

Ah Pau didn't answer me, but kept weeping.

Auntie came over and pointed to the backyard and said, "I asked someone to find that for you. It's very difficult to find one this time of year."

There was a small lichee tree in the corner of the courtyard. The roots of the tree were wrapped in burlap. "You bought it for me, Auntie? But why?"

Auntie didn't know how to answer me, and neither did Ah Pau. Kee took a bag of something from behind his back and said simply, "For you."

"What's that?"

"Open it and see."

I opened it. I was stunned and for a long time I couldn't say a word. There were my lichees. Kee had taken them without my permission! I screamed, "Why did you pick my lichees?"

Kee didn't say a word. He just looked at Ah Pau, as if asking for help. Ah Pau didn't know what to say. It made me even angrier, because she hadn't prevented Kee from picking my lichees. I was as mad as a hornet. I cried and yelled and didn't listen. "You stole my lichees! Put them back on the tree for me! You put them back on the tree for me!"

I started kicking and hitting him, but he didn't fight back or defend himself. He just stood there, while Ah Pau tried her best to pull me away from him. I screamed, "It serves you right for your father and sister to run away!"

Someone slapped me. It was Kee. Touching my cheek, I expected Ah Pau to scold him. But instead she shouted angrily, "How dare you say that? Do you want me to slap you, too!"

What in the world! Kee stole my lichees and slapped me, and Ah Pau was shouting at me and even wanted to slap me, too! They were treating me like an enemy! With my hand covering my cheek, I ran toward the door.

I was stopped and embraced by Auntie, who was standing at the door. "Calm down, young lady. Calm down."

Feeling Auntie was the only person in the world who loved me and cared about me, I let her gently pat my back.

"Come sit down and have a cup of tea. You will feel better." I let Auntie walk me to the daybed.

Kee at once brought me a cup of tea. Ah Pau brought me a towel to wipe my face. After I drank the tea, I felt better.

Ah Pau sat next to me. She took some lichees out of the bag and said, "These are not your lichees. Look, yours are much bigger than these."

She was right. They didn't look like my lichees—mine were much bigger and prettier.

In a low voice, Ah Pau said, "I tried to tell you, but you wouldn't listen."

I was quiet.

Ah Pau continued, "Kee bought them just for you. He didn't even buy any for himself."

I said to Kee, "I'm sorry. But you knew I was going to pick my lichees. Why did you buy these for me?"

Kee looked at Ah Pau again as if asking her to help him. Ah Pau held my hand and said, "You are a big girl now. I have something to tell you. You must promise not to yell or scream like you did just a moment ago."

"I'm sorry." I lowered my head, ashamed of myself.

Ah Pau let out a sigh and said, "We have to move back here."

"Why?" I jerked my head up and looked at her. "How about our new house?"

"Our new house—" Ah Pau paused. "The new house doesn't belong to us anymore."

"How about my lichee tree?" I jumped up from the daybed and ran toward the door before they could stop me.

I was at the new house in seconds. The door was open, as usual. I didn't have time to look in the living room. I went straight to the backyard, where I saw Ghost Walk and several other people talking and eating my lichees. One man was still up in my tree! I used all my strength to kick Ghost Walk's skinny rear. Before he had time to turn around to see what was going on, I kicked another man's rear.

Kee had followed me and tried his best to pull me away. I struggled wildly. Ah Pau was there, too, crying and trying to help Kee pull me back. Twisting and tugging, I tried to look back at the group of people. I yelled as loud as I could, "You will die for eating my lichees! You will die for eating my lichees!"

27

"Please eat just a few bites," Ah Pau begged me, holding a bowl of rice in front of me. But I pushed it away.

"I'm not hungry," I said.

"How about a couple of lichees? Ah Mei and Ah Won bought several for you, in addition to Kee's. You have to eat them before they completely turn dark."

"I'm not hungry."

"You haven't eaten anything for two days," Ah Pau said worriedly. "If you don't eat, you will get sick, and you'll miss more school. Kee promised to take you out to find snails or whatever you want to do after final exams."

"I don't want to go out. I don't want Hing Kee's owner to say that I was fooling him."

"It's not your fault. Everybody in town knows that Ghost Walk got our store and our house," Auntie said. She couldn't keep from coughing.

"We didn't need to give our store and new house to

him," I said, leaning on the daybed and feeling weak.

"You don't understand, Ying. Your uncle knew that sooner or later, Ghost Walk would set fire to the store like he did to Ah Yee's house."

"Ah Yee's house?"

"Yes. They found a kerosene bottle around their house, but no one would say a word."

"Why not?"

Ah Pau sighed. "Everybody is scared of Ghost Walk. Everybody is afraid that he will take revenge. But your uncle is a kind man. He thought that if Ghost Walk set fire to our store, it would also ruin the bookstore and carpenter shop on either side. It would create a disaster for the whole town. We have had bad luck, but Uncle didn't want other people to have bad luck because of us."

"Why did he have to go away?"

"He didn't want to. Auntie and I urged him to go. We knew Ghost Walk wouldn't give up easily. He would torture Uncle like he did Ah Yee's father. He would make up things and do cruel things to Uncle as revenge for not letting Ah So be his second concubine."

"But it's not fair to me. I didn't do anything wrong, and he took my tree."

"We know it's unfair to you, but there was nothing we could do about it," Ah Pau said, pulling a strand of hair away from my forehead.

"I could! I could have guarded my tree all day long and all night long and not let them have it."

"You are too young, Ying. It would be like an egg hitting a rock. You know what happens to the egg."

"At least I would have picked all the lichees earlier so they couldn't have any. Why didn't you tell me sooner?"

Ah Pau sighed again, and said, "That's my fault. When Ghost Walk told Auntie that he was going to take our new house if we didn't turn in more money and gold within ten days, I thought he was just threatening us. I thought nobody would do that kind of thing, since we had already given him all our valuable belongings, and Uncle had left our family. But I was also afraid he really meant it. He had seen your lichee tree. It would only aggravate him if he found out that the tree had been picked. That's why I told you to leave it alone. I didn't want to upset you before I knew if he really meant it." Ah Pau wept again.

I didn't comfort her this time because I was very sad. "I have tried, Ah Pau. I have tried hard to help you find Uncle."

"I know. You are a sweet girl, but we have just had a very bad year. Still, we are going to be okay."

"I wish Ghost Walk was dead! I wish the thunder god would strike him!"

"Nobody can punish him but the heaven god," Ah Pau said. "Let's not talk about him. It's over. The new house, the tree, the store, are material things. We still have each other. We can start again. We can plant another tree."

"I don't want to plant another one," I said quietly.

"How about eating first," Ah Pau said more energetically than before. "Try Kee's *bok choi*. It's not big, but it is fresh and tender."

"Where did Kee get the *bok choi*?"

"I replanted it after you ruined mine. I swore I wouldn't let you have a bite, but I've changed my mind."

I had never thought Kee would replant the *bok choi*.

"Here, eat it." Ah Pau picked up a few green leaves of *bok choi* with the chopsticks and said, "After you eat, we can plant that lichee tree. It has been out there for a couple of days already. It will die if you don't plant it soon."

"I can help you dig the hole," Kee said voluntarily.

Kee was being so nice to me, even in the tone of his voice. So I let Ah Pau put the *bok choi* into my mouth. It was very tender and sweet. They were very happy that I ate.

"I am sorry for ruining your *bok choi,* Kee. I never thought that you would plant it again."

"I didn't want to at first, but Grandma encouraged me. What was it you said, Grandma?"

"Well, I cannot read or write, but I have learned how to survive. If something is gone, I try not to mourn over it. I start over. If things break, I don't just throw them away. I fix them. If things are going very badly, I look forward to the turning point. I know there must always be a turning point. I wouldn't have lived for seven decades if I did not think this way. Anyway, I am glad Kee listened to me. Now his *bok choi* can help us at least for a little while."

"That means . . . I should plant the tree?"

"I would if I were you," said Ah Pau.

"If I plant the tree, I will be fifteen before I can get another lichee harvest! It will be a long, long time!"

"Just blink your eyes and you will be fifteen, young lady." Ah Pau said, putting another bite of *bok choi* into my mouth.

After eating, I felt much stronger. Kee started to dig a hole in the middle of the backyard. The yard was not as big as the one at the new house. After he dug the hole, the sky was getting dark. Ah Pau held a kerosene lamp while Kee helped me place the tree and fill the hole with dirt.

"I hope this one is as good as the other one, Auntie," I said, watering the tree.

"I hope so, too. My friend who found the tree for me said it is a good variety."

"I will buy you a tree to plant when I get the money from this tree, Auntie. I promise."

Auntie didn't say anything. She just smiled. Kee didn't bark at me for my "empty talk."

"After we get the lichees from this tree, I can still help you find Uncle, and I can even take Auntie to see the doctor."

"I hope I don't need to wait that long to be able to see Uncle, and Auntie's cough will be gone by then."

"Can I use the money to build another new house?"

"Oh," Ah Pau smiled. She patted my head and said,

"It'll take a lot of money to build a new house."

"I can save the money each year to build it, can't I?"

"You can do whatever you want," Kee said. I couldn't believe it was Kee talking.

"Are you going to bury a dead cat next to this tree, Ah Pau?"

"Sure, as soon as I can find one. It's the best fertilizer."

"Can I start to dig the hole for the cat, now?"

"Wait until I find the dead cat first."

"I want to dig one now, so when you have the cat, I can just bury it."

"Just let her dig it. She hasn't been out of the house for two days and has so much energy," Auntie said from inside, using a palm fan to shoo away the mosquitos.

Ah Pau gave up and was ready to go back inside. She said, "Don't dig too close to the roots."

Despite the mosquitos, I put the kerosene lamp on the ground and found a spot, asking, "Is it far enough from the roots, Ah Pau?"

"I think so."

I started digging. It was not as easy as I had thought.

"Let me start a little hole for you. The dirt is hard," Kee offered.

"I can do it," I said. But the hoe kept bouncing off and wouldn't go deep down in the soil.

"You don't have much strength. Are you sure you don't need help?"

"Yes. I want to do it myself."

"Why don't you come back inside, eat some lichees, and rest for a while first," Auntie suggested.

"I don't want to," I said quietly. I felt my eyes begin to get moist again. I blinked my eyes hard and declared, "I don't want to eat any lichees this year."

Auntie understood. She didn't suggest it again.

Kee interrupted, "Just keep digging in the same place, and pretty soon it will become a hole." He left to go inside.

So I started digging again. I suddenly heard the hoe hit something that made a *crack*. "No wonder! There is a rock underneath here, Ah Pau! I am going to change to another spot!"

"Try not to make too many holes in the yard," Ah Pau said.

"Okay," I said and started to dig again.

Crack!

I complained, "It's still a rock, Ah Pau."

"Okay, you can dig at another spot."

As I just raised up the hoe and was ready to start another hole, I spotted something black in the place where I had dug before. I moved the kerosene lamp and lowered my head to have a closer look. "What is that?"

"What is what?" Ah Pau asked from inside.

"I don't know—some black stuff underneath some broken clay."

I didn't expect Ah Pau and Auntie to both rush out. Ah Pau almost tripped. "Let me see, let me see!" she said. Then she cried out, "That's *it*!"

Auntie also let out a cry of joy.

"What is it?" Kee rushed out, dumping a lichee seed in the yard.

"It's the jar of silver coins we have been looking for all over the house!" Ah Pau grinned.

"How come they are black? I thought silver is supposed to be white," Kee asked.

"They are tarnished," Ah Pau said.

"Are we rich now, Ah Pau?"

"At least we won't be hungry for a while."

"Can you go find Uncle?"

"Sure. But I want Auntie to see the doctor first. Go find me a spade."

Kee found it for Ah Pau. I got two stools for Auntie and Ah Pau to sit down on.

"It has been so many years ago that I didn't even remember where I had buried it." Ah Pau was overjoyed.

"Don't anyone breathe a word about this. Otherwise Ghost Walk will accuse us of not turning over everything to him," Auntie warned us.

"It's the right time and the right place," Ah Pau said. "I told you there would be a turning point, didn't I?"

I smiled at Ah Pau. "Yes, you did."

GLOSSARY

abacus — Traditional Chinese manual calculator.

aiyah — Chinese exclamation.

Baba — Father.

bok choi — Leafy Chinese vegetable used in stir-frying or making soup.

bride price — A gift that the groom's family offers to the bride's family before they get married.

catty — A unit of measurement equal to approximately one and one-third pounds.

century egg — Preserved duck egg.

cicada — A dark brown insect that makes a shrill sound in the spring and summer.

concubine — A secondary wife with inferior social and legal status.

coolie — A laborer who transports goods.

dai gut lai see — A Chinese expression meaning the same as "knock on wood."

fohgei — A worker who helps in stores or restaurants.

kung kung — Maternal grandfather.

kwailo — "Foreign devil," a name used for male Caucasians.

lichee tree — A tree that grows in warm climates such as southeastern China. It produces fruit about the size of Ping-pong balls, with a rough, reddish peel. Inside is a juicy, sweet white pulp around a small, brown seed.

Moon Festival — An important Chinese festival celebrated in mid-autumn, when families come together for a reunion meal. Celebrants worship a legendary beauty, Chang-O, who flew to the moon where she lives with a white rabbit.

sau jau — Woven cylindrical wrist protectors worn by rice farmers during rice harvest.

tong cheong sam — Traditional southeastern Chinese tunic.

tong cheong hai — Soft, strapless shoes made out of black material, usually worn by men.

yeen ji — Something like a Hackey Sack made of feathers and stacks of cut round paper that people kick for fun.